G000150324

How Will You Remember Me?

Janine Cobain

Write Path NI Limited

HOW WILL YOU REMEMBER ME?

Copyright © 2014 Janine Cobain. All rights reserved.

First paperback edition printed 2014 in the United Kingdom.

A catalogue record for this book is available from the British Library.

ISBN 978-0-9927824-4-3

No part of this book shall be reproduced or transmitted in any form or by any means, electronic or mechanical, including photocopying, recording, or by any information retrieval system without written permission of the publisher.

Published by Write Path NI Limited

For more copies of this book, please email:
info@writepathni.com

Cover designed by Write Path NI Limited

Original Artwork by Sue Green

Printed in Great Britain

Although every precaution has been taken in the preparation of this book, the publisher and author assume no responsibility for errors or omissions. Neither is any liability assumed for damages resulting from the use of this information contained herein.

To everyone I have known in my life; thank you. Each of you have given me inspiration in some way — an emotion, an experience, an idea, or a dream — it all helped to give life to this book, and its characters.

Special thanks to my husband, Steve, for his unfailing support, and for always being on speed-dial.

Janine x

CONTENTS

Acknowledgement

For you; remember me?

CHAPTER 1

It was October when the call came. A low autumn sun beamed from a glorious blue sky, its chilly breath whispering a promise of dark, cosy nights. My favourite kind of day. When the nurse delivered the news, it stopped my heart. Just for a moment.

My Husband was dead.

The words tumbled around my head. I thanked her, closed my eyes, and allowed the news to filter from my ear to my brain. I waited, braced for the ache of grief to build in that sweet spot between the heart and gut. It didn't come.

Technically, legally, he was someone else's husband. He hadn't been mine for seven years. Jack was Laura's mess now. The grief, rightfully, hers. I stared at my expressionless reflection in the rear view mirror. Tear-free, blue eyes. Cold, hardened. I pushed the car into gear and finished the drive home.

I locked the car as I walked away, across the

underground car park, and headed for the lift. I was on the top floor, the 'penthouse suite' Jessica would say. I called it the flat, partly to wind her up, but mostly because apartment sounded pretentious, and, no matter what my bank balance said, I was still a working class girl from the north of England.

I twisted the key in the lock, pushed my weight against the door, and marched into the kitchen. Dumping my bags on the island, I headed for the fridge. I needed to tell someone, and I needed a drink. Neither had a higher priority, so I did both. I selected Jessica's number from my recent calls as I decanted wine into a large glass.

"Hi Cath, are you on your way?" Jessica answered.

We met at university and instantly bonded, best friends forever. I knew her mannerisms so well, I could see her now, smiling as she spoke, her mobile held in place with her shoulder, stirring something on the hob with one hand and reaching for an ingredient with the other.

"Not yet, I stopped off to change." I felt awkward. How should I break the news, did I need to display some sensitivity? "So, Jack's dead."

A pause. Things were stiller at the other end of the line.

"When?"

"Just, hospice rang."

"Are you okay Catherine? I mean, really okay?"

I knew what she was asking. Was I okay under the layer of armour I had worn since I left him.

"I am, but I need a drink."

"Leave the car there, I'll send Andrew for you."

I adored Andrew. They had married when she returned to Belfast armed with her degree from Newcastle University. He was fair, with dark eyes, tall — much taller than my 5'8" — and still carried the build from his days playing rugby. One of his hugs made the world feel like a safer place. The physical contrast between him and his wife was almost comical. She was short and slender, with shoulder-length, dark brown hair that glinted auburn in sunlight.

Filled with dread I called Jack's wife.

"Cath, Oh God, Cath, he's gone," Laura sobbed. "I asked the nurse to call; I couldn't say the words... I was cutting up his dinner, and he just fell back and..." Her words dissolved.

"Laura, I am so sorry."

The ache was building, pushing against my ribs, and tears blurred my vision. I closed my eyes. Laura was devastated, left with a huge hole in her life and a child not yet five. She sounded like she would cry forever. Whatever had gone on between Jack and I was immaterial, she loved him. One of the things I struggled with, in the early days, was we wouldn't be together when we died. I pushed the thought away.

"I'm glad you were with him, at the end."

Andrew announced his arrival by text as I hung up. I kicked off my shoes and pulled my dress off over my head with one hand, lifting a clean t-shirt and jogging pants from the wardrobe with the other. I dressed quickly, pulled my hair into a ponytail, and pushed my feet into well-worn trainers. I needed comfort; this was a start. I drained the wine glass and headed down to my chauffeur.

Andrew was at the passenger door of his car and whistled as I jogged to his open arms.

"I see you made an effort for me," he mocked, enveloping me in his big arms, and placing a tender kiss on my forehead. I breathed in the aroma of him. People's scent had always fascinated me. My Grandmother was convinced that my sense of smell was heightened because I was destined to lose one of my other senses. He smelt good - Molton Brown — Heavenly Gingerlilly.

"You've been stealing your wife's shower gel again," I remarked.

"I'm in touch with my feminine side, there's nothing wrong with that!" He laughed, and opened the car door for me.

We drove through the teatime traffic, and pulled into their driveway. 'Writer's Rest' was a cream-rendered, detached house, nestled in acres of rolling green on the southern outskirts of Belfast. Triangular floods of light beamed down from the eaves, illuminating it in a soft, welcoming light.

Jessica was waiting with a hug at the kitchen door. She excelled in these situations, overflowing with sympathy and understanding, and although I didn't need either, I let her cluck around me.

"You're bound to feel something Cat; you were together a long time. You've spent more of your life with him than without him," Jessica reasoned, as she cleared my plate and topped up my glass.

I shrugged and looked for a suitable response in the bottom of my wine glass, swirling the contents. Was I deluding myself? Perhaps I was in shock and the grief would hit me at an inopportune moment. I frowned, I had some important events in the next few weeks, and it would be annoying if I crumbled into some lamenting mess.

"Auntie Cath!"

I surfaced from my thoughts. "Hello Sweetheart."

Lucy, Jessica and Andrew's daughter, bounced to my side, and threw her hands around my neck. Her long tawny hair tickled my nose as I inhaled the strawberry sweetness of her. She was my god-daughter, and the nearest thing I was likely to get to a child of my own. At thirty-nine years old, that ship had sailed.

Children had been part of the plan. The original plan, the one that involved Jack and me living happily ever after. We met as teenagers, drawn together by youthful exuberance and passion. We finished our respective schooling, before I went on to university locally and Jack got a job in construction. We plodded along without any major dramas, it was an amicable relationship, and even though we had little in common, it worked. We worked.

We married in a simple ceremony with close friends as witnesses. My parents had died long before, leaving my older sister, Elizabeth, and me in the care of our Grandparents. Jack's father was rarely invited to social events; he was a drinker, and foul with it. We moved into our new home, a spacious semi-detached house in leafy suburbia, the plan unspoken, but obvious. We would have children, and grandchildren, and would, undoubtedly, live happily ever after.

And it started out well. Within three months of our marriage, the seeds of our happiness were planted and our love for each other swelled with my stomach. Twenty weeks in to what had been a dream pregnancy, I awoke one morning to painful stomach cramps, then blood, and then a baby boy born far too early to survive.

We were offered no support, no counselling, and no reason for our loss. We were distraught, with nothing and no one to blame, but ourselves. I was entrusted with the safekeeping of our precious child, and I had failed. In time, Jack found it easier to blame me, and with no other outlet for his grief, it manifested into an ugly anger. He found solace in drink, as his father had. With alcohol blurring his sense of right and wrong, he lashed out, again as his father had before him, first at doors, and then smashing things in pure frustration, splintering them into a thousand pieces.

It was only a matter of time before he directed his attention to me. I needed his love, his comfort, and instead I got his venom. It culminated in an explosion of violence, blows rained down on me and I curled in to a foetal position, to protect myself, as he punched and kicked out at me.

I forgave, but never forgot. Time did its best to heal, but I was unwilling to surrender to the vulnerability of pregnancy again, and buried myself in my work. Jack was working long hours too, but he drowned his grief in drink before discovering cocaine, replacing the feel good high, we used to get from each other, with a chemical alternative he didn't need to nurture.

Our relationship had changed beyond all recognition and I had known, of course I'd known. Didn't we always? If not by admission then by default? The cuckoo in the nest was always evident, even if not openly discussed, or acknowledged. Her existence had been evident by Jack's behaviour. His absences, his lack of interest in us, by the care he took in his appearance. It was evident by the new aftershave, the sickly sweet smell of Obsession exuded from him before their encounters. The investment in the new car, a sleek silver number with a leather interior and alloy wheels. What mistress would want to be chauffeured around in his old work van?

Even when confronted he had denied it, and had placated me with clichés, 'Why would I? I have everything I want in you'. The cuckoo was a friend. Less than that, she was the friend of a friend, a barmaid in his newly favourite haunt. He had taken me there a few months earlier, brazenly now it transpired, and pointed her out. Physically she had reminded me of my younger self, and I had known she wanted him by her cool indifference.

A woman knows.

At first, I naively assumed it was a one way longing, that our history would be enough for him to revel in the flattery of the attraction of a young thing, without breaking the bonds of matrimony. I had mentioned my observation to him and he had laughed. We had laughed.

How wrong, how foolish. How misguided of me to trust that our vows would be more powerful than the surge of heat in his pants.

And so, there we were, six months into their relationship and a bastard child was revealed as his heir. At the moment of revelation, of confirmation, I felt nothing but euphoria. I was right, I had always been right. This infidelity wasn't a figment of my crazed imagination, as it had been portrayed. I was relieved. My instincts were true, and the tension left me. I wasn't deluded, or twisted.

I had just known.

CHAPTER 2

I lifted my small suitcase from under the desk and scanned the office. The glass exterior wall offered an uninterrupted view of City Hall, an impressive milky-stoned construction at the heart of the city. I remembered driving up to it on my arrival in Belfast and asking the taxi driver to stop, so I could take a photograph. It was dark, the structure was illuminated with beams of blue, and white fairy lights draped through the trees in the grounds. It looked magical, and I wanted to preserve the feeling of awe, from when I first laid eyes on it, forever. In the light of day, the smudged scars from the traffic fumes were obvious, and some of the enchantment was lost, but the magnificence was still evident.

Here, in the comfort of my black leather office

chair, I was content. Everything had been chosen carefully. The shelves built into the wall behind me housed the books, files, and magazines I used for reference, a teak desk, made to suit my height, curved around me. The horseshoe conference table curled in front of the window on the plush grey carpet, the plum corner sofa edged the room behind the door, and an exquisite Terry Bradley original hung vibrant against the smooth wall. A door behind the desk led to a small dressing room and bathroom that had proved invaluable in the early days, when I often pulled twenty-hour working days. I undocked the laptop, slipped it into my bag, and lifted my mobile. Locking the office door, I pulled the case behind me, down in the lift, to the luxurious lobby of Catherine Harvey Promotions. Jenny, our pristine receptionist, sat behind the sweeping red desk.

"Jenny, I've cleared my diary so there should be no visitors for me the rest of the week. I won't be available tomorrow on my mobile until after, say, 2pm. Lisa will take any messages."

"No worries, safe trip Miss Harvey."

It still amused me that Jenny called me Miss Harvey at work, when she had seen me worse for wear on more than one occasion, and had crashed at my flat several times. She was an asset to the company, a people-person, smart and intelligent. All my staff were assets, competent in their positions, and hired so I could step back and enjoy the fruits of my labour, and take an interest in projects that fed my soul.

We had zero staff turnover, I had a knack of

choosing good people, and not only did they have excellent pay packages, they were my work family and I treated them as such. Their problems were shared, their successes celebrated and in whatever way they needed the support of the company, or me, they had it. They rewarded me with loyalty and hard work, and that seemed like a fair trade.

I climbed in to the waiting taxi, sitting in the back to avoid conversation, and directed him to Belfast City airport. I called Jessica. She had offered to accompany me to Jack's funeral, but I wanted to do this alone. I didn't know why, it seemed right.

Jessica had thrown me a lifeline, and summoned me to Belfast, when I left Jack. It had proved to be a good move. She had taken over her father's publishing business, after his death, and wanted to pull it into the 21st Century. Ulster Press had been my first client, and, as instructed, I went through it with a fine toothcomb. Recommending new practices, designing procedures, putting together operation manuals, training staff, and highlighting the importance of service, not only to the stockists, but also to nurturing the authors who were the lifeblood of the business, and who deserved to be cherished. I took over the marketing and promotion of new publications, organised book launches, readings, and signings. Jessica's authors did well in the best-seller lists, and so others hired me too. The thing about Northern Ireland is everyone knows someone you know, and a recommendation is worth more than any advertisement. Catherine Harvey Promotions earned a solid reputation for good, productive service, and the business flourished.

I adored my adopted home, not only the city, but also the country, the people, the buildings, the craic — everything. Having grown the business over the last seven years, our offices in the heart of the city were testament to its success, and nothing happened in the north of this beautiful island without CHP being involved somewhere. We turned our hand to anything.

Arriving at the airport, I sailed through security and settled in Starbucks with a large, black coffee. The screen told me to 'Relax and Shop' for another 12 minutes. I browsed the company twitter account, aimlessly blowing the surface of my drink. We had over two hundred thousand followers, and a small social media team who answered every tweet, handled each request, and responded to all the enquiries. I believed in exceeding expectations in everything I did, and customer service in our industry was paramount to success. Failure was not an option. Not anymore.

Gate 18. I ditched my coffee and followed the signs, exchanging pleasantries with familiar faces. This was classic Northern Ireland; if you believed in the concept of 'Six Degrees of Separation', here it was three. Boarded and buckled up, I switched off my mobile and relaxed back into my seat, letting my mind drift.

The barmaid hadn't lasted long. As Jack found out to his cost, young girls play games and she wasn't pregnant, it was just a ruse to get him to leave his marriage. It was too late for us; I was long gone. He met Laura soon after and they were happy, with a beautiful daughter who was the apple of her daddy's eye. Jack was a different man with Laura. I was a rocky coastline that he crashed against, she was a sandy beach, smooth and welcoming, that he washed over. He didn't need the drink, or drugs to get him through the day. I was as much to blame for the breakdown in our marriage as he was. We had made our peace and I wished them well. It was for the best; we had both grown and found happiness. A cruel twist of fate had seen him diagnosed with terminal cancer a few months ago, and the end had been swift.

I mulled over Jessica's observation — that I should feel something — but, in truth, I didn't. Not for me, anyway. I felt sad for his wife and daughter, and for his family. I neither loved nor hated him, so I felt nothing, and no amount of overthinking was going to change that. When I remembered our life, I recalled the pain, the infidelity, the failure. Memories of happier times were buried beneath a layer of thorns.

I picked up the hire car from Newcastle airport and drove down the A1, smiling at the landmarks of my former home. The Metro Centre, the Angel of the North, and the industrial estate where I had worked in a previous life. Almost an hour after landing, I pulled into the car park of the hotel nearest to St. Patrick's Church, where tomorrow's service was to be held. I had stayed in some incredible hotels around the world, the peak of luxury, with glorious views, and fabulous amenities, but there was something instantly comfortable, and familiar, about the purple welcome of a Premier Inn.

I hung my dress in the bathroom and turned on the shower to let the steam loosen the creases. Peering into the mirror, I pulled the skin tight across my face. Shame the steam couldn't work its magic on me. In fairness, I wasn't doing too badly, a combination of good living and great skincare. I stepped into the welcome stream of hot water and let it flow over me, pushing it back off my face before turning my back to it. I squeezed the Imperial Leather hair and body wash from the wall-mounted holder, and the clean scent took me back to my Nana's bathroom of my childhood.

Wrapped in a towel, I poured wine into a glass from the bathroom, and made myself comfortable on the big bed, positioning the sumptuous pillows around me. I flicked on the television. Even though I had only been gone seven years, hearing my accent on the news was strange, and I preferred the delicious tones of those native to Northern Ireland. Once dry, I climbed under the duvet and set my alarm for 8am, not that I slept late, but if I were ever going to it would be tomorrow.

CHAPTER 3

The day of the funeral dawned bright, clear, and unseasonably warm. I debated leaving my jacket, but those lofty catholic churches could get cold.

Breakfast was a self-service affair. I poured myself coffee and juice, and filled a plate with bacon, sausages, and scrambled eggs. I didn't trust myself with beans; I always managed to feed my cleavage. In fairness it would be hard to miss, and, even if I did say so myself, it was sitting well today. God bless Marks and Spencer's lingerie department. I finished my caffeine fix, checked emails, and silenced the phone before dropping it in my handbag.

It was a short car journey; the crowd, gathered outside, marked the location. Jack had been popular in his time, although in recent years he had mixed with a new circle of friends. How many of his old friends would have known he was even sick, never mind dead?

I waited on the steps of the church, mouthing a 'Hi' and waving acknowledgements to Jack's family and friends who I recognised, and as the hearse pulled up I made my way inside. I wasn't sure of the protocol as to where to sit at your ex-husbands funeral, and so I plumbed for the middle on the right, well back from his family and close friends.

The funeral procession made its way up the aisle, and placed the coffin up front. Still, I felt nothing. Laura sobbed, and Jack's brother and sister were united in their grief. Cousins, aunties and uncles, friends, all of them tearful. I felt a bit of a fraud. Should I try to force a tear, would that be more acceptable?

The priest began the service, as he had a thousand times before, and I zoned out, taking in the surroundings behind the altar, the decorative stained-glass windows, and magnificently ornate alcoves. I followed the architectural line of the ceiling in an arc down the pillar to my right, and I saw him. Not Jack, obviously, him.

Seated on a pew, a few in front of me — a little way to the right — he was half turned in his seat. His black suit jacket stretched across his broad shoulders, and the top button of his shirt was open, his tie slightly skewed. He looked as though he would be more comfortable in a t-shirt and combats. He stared intently at the priest, taking in every word, mouthing responses. He was around forty, his dark hair was shaved close to his head, a beard, no more than stubble, peppered his handsome face. He appeared focused on Father O'Brien, but his piercing blue eyes scanned the congregation. The crowd rose to sing a hymn, and I watched him unfurl. He cut a fine figure from behind. Good legs and tall, well over six foot, and I found myself wondering, as I always did with tall men, whether he was in proportion. I had the decency to blush at the thought, and at the feelings stirring deep inside. A draft carried the scent of him to me and, like a vampire catching fresh blood on the breeze, my stomach tightened, the citrus notes of his aftershave teased my senses. Delicious. I shook my head. I should be ashamed, drooling over a stranger at my ex-husbands funeral.

I was so going to Hell.

The taxi pulled to a halt outside the church.

"This is you, mate," the taxi driver announced, stopping the meter. Connor paid the fare, waving away the offer of change, and stepped out into the warm October morning. He smoothed down his jacket, and loosened his tie, undoing the top button of the shirt. He had spent too long in this suit in recent days; it was depressing, and uncomfortable. There was quite a gathering, and he scanned the unfamiliar crowd, not expecting to recognise anyone. The guy he knew was coming up the road in a hearse. Connor hoped she would be there, the shy, dark-haired girl from the photograph. She would be twenty years older than in the grainy image. Would he recognise her? He wanted to give her the picture, and pass on

Jack's message.

He entered the cool respite of the church and took a seat, appraising each woman as she passed by. None resembled the girl from the photograph. Connor followed the service, responding, and dropping his head in the right places. He could do this in his sleep.

Was she here? He rose, for the hymn, and turned to look over his shoulder. No sign of the target, but the sight that greeted him was a pleasing one. Connor was a good judge of people, his life had often depended on it, and this woman had a visible strength, evident here when every other female in the church was crying, she was dry-eyed. Yes, there was a tension in her face, but her eyes were dancing. She wore confidence like a perfume. He could smell it. It was in the well-cut clothes, the lightly styled hair, and minimal make-up. It was good to see skin tone on a woman's face, rather than an orange tidemark framing it. It was refreshing; she was refreshing. Tall with curves in all the right places. She was flushed, and he wondered if that was what she would look like with a post-coital glow. She leaned forward to retrieve her handbag, and, unwittingly, gave him a perfect view of her ample cleavage. She raised her head and met his appreciative stare. She smirked and locked her eyes on his. His breath caught in his throat and he averted his gaze. What was he thinking? He was in church for Christ's sake!

He was so going to Hell.

Jack's cousins lifted the coffin to the strains of a song billed as being by one of his favourite groups.

18

As I filed out of the church, I recognised the music. It was one of his favourites, and had invoked the spectre of him whenever I heard it over the years. Dumbfounded, I kept my face straight. Was this chosen on purpose, or had someone missed the irony of playing 'Going Underground' as he was about to be buried?

You couldn't write this shit!

Standing in the crowd on the church steps, as the coffin was loaded for its final journey, I recognised the voice muttering behind me.

"Did you see the order of service? 'Gods will'? It is the will of God, there's a bloody apostrophe!"

"Fiona, how are you?" I asked, and embraced my ex-sister-in-law with genuine affection. I had missed her friendship since I evacuated, and her irritation at the missing punctuation reminded me.

"As well as can be expected? Isn't that the standard response?" Fiona said, returning my hug. "And don't even start me on the choice of music, what the fuck was she thinking?"

Fiona wasn't a fan of her new sister-in-law. In truth, she was barely a fan of her brother's, after his infidelity. We had been good friends, sisters even, but distance and time had diluted the relationship, although we had never fallen out. The thing I liked most about her was what others disliked, her straightness. She was direct, almost to the point of rudeness, and would not tolerate stupidity, nor make allowances for it. She had a hard shell and was brutal at times, but she was honest and loyal, qualities I valued.

"What about you?" Fiona asked.

"I'm fine. This all feels a little strange, but I wanted to come."

"To make sure the bastard was dead?" She asked, laughing.

I shushed her, suppressing a chuckle. "Behave," I cautioned, "I'm already struggling to keep my warped sense of humour in check. I don't need encouragement from you!"

"Come on, you can drive me to the cemetery," she said, linking my arm with hers. "Those funeral cars are depressing. You can fill me in on your recent sexploits. Mine have been dreary of late."

I hung back away from the grave, uncomfortable walking over the resting place of others. It felt disrespectful. It allowed me to gather my thoughts, ever the analyst. I had a bouquet of memories, some were fragrant and beautiful, and others had thorns. I wanted to be able to lift the pleasant ones by the stem, enjoy the recollection and replace it, without cutting myself on the ones that hurt.

Whenever I revisited memories of my life with Jack it was the violence, the adultery, the awfulness of everything that came to mind first. I wanted to remember the good times, the fun. The times we shared before we died inside. It had never been possible, but seeing Fiona today was helping a little with the navigation of the complex blooms.

The day after the funeral, I woke feeling rested and content. I had buried the past, literally, and the curtains to my future had been pulled back with gusto. I thought of him, the mystery man. He had unnerved me. His eyes had burned into me and lit a fuse deep inside. A man hadn't stirred me like that for a long time; emotionally, I had closed off. Don't misunderstand me; I wasn't in training for the sisterhood by any stretch of the imagination. I was enthusiastically heterosexual, but I viewed liaisons as stress relief, almost like a visit to the gym. You worked hard, built up a sweat, and the endorphins released kept you buoyant until the next session. It was good for the mental health; sexual frustration did not sit well on me.

I had some good male friends who I could call on to accompany me to a function, visit the cinema, or go for a meal, or a drink, but they were strictly platonic. It was cringe worthy even to consider letting them see me naked, let alone engage in anything else. I had, for want of a better description, a 'fuck buddy'. We met at a conference in Derry, years ago, and after a successful night, fuelled by alcohol, had discovered we clicked. Outside of it, we wouldn't have given each other a second glance, and neither of us wanted anything more than an itch scratched, so it suited us. Only ever a phone call away, Jessica had christened him 'Speed-dial Steve'.

On the return flight to Belfast, relaxed by a glass of Cabernet Sauvignon in the airport, I found myself thinking about Mr Mystery in ways I hadn't thought about a man in a long time. I was used to strange ideas drifting in to my head, and forming like candyfloss, spinning slowly gathering strands, until they gained shape and bulk, but this was an unfamiliar concept. I thought about his lips, and how he would taste. I thought about his hair, and how it would feel under my fingers. I thought about the stubble on his chin grazing the inside of my thigh.

Shit.

I sat upright and looked around at my fellow passengers, worried my fantasy was so real they would read my mind. What was the matter with me? I was confused; this wasn't me. I was focused, driven, and organised, not some whimsical fantasist who had rude thoughts about a stranger.

Was this my grief? Jessica had counselled it was a personal emotion that people reacted to in their own way. I would bet money no one else's 'way' was to fixate on some hot guy they had seen at their husband's funeral. EX husband. Past tense. I would Google it when I got home. Google was my friend; he would have the answer. If he didn't, Jessica would, and if she didn't, well, Speed-dial Steve would deal with the itch.

CHAPTER 4

Three weeks after my return from England and I still felt... what... Odd? Odd was a good word. I felt odd. I couldn't pinpoint what was wrong, and while I knew I wasn't grieving, I hadn't decided what I was feeling.

October was always a busy month with back to back book launches as publishers vied for the Christmas market share, and, now they were all done, we had a lull before the madness of Christmas set upon us. Gathered around the conference table in my office I had told the management team I would be taking a couple of weeks out for some 'me' time, which they met with good-natured grumbles. I had decided to take the break five minutes before the meeting, but it was a good idea.

I called Lisa in. "I'm going to head up to the cottage, could you call and ask the caretaker to switch the heating on please?"

"Sure, would you like me to see if Mr Friday is available to join you?" Lisa wasn't even trying to be funny; 'Speed-Dial Steve' was better known as Mr Steve Friday. The irony was never lost on me.

"No, thanks. I'm going solo."

I moved to the rain-splattered window, and looked out onto the grey November day; its coldness permeated the glass. I relaxed; this time tomorrow, I would be in the cottage, with a log fire blazing, a glass of something mildly alcoholic, and a trashy film. Instantly I felt warmer, happier, and I looked down to the street below.

And there he was.

He pressed the button at the crossing, along from City Hall, and waited. It couldn't be, could it? I pressed against the cold glass and peered hard. I was four floors up, but I had 'seen' this man in my dreams and fantasies for weeks. It was him. The lights changed and he crossed the road, disappearing from my line of sight. What should I do? I wanted to bang on the window and scream, run down the stairs, out into the street and yell for him to wait. With a crushing resignation, I knew it was ridiculous to think it was him.

"You need to get a grip," I scolded myself. Defeated, I slumped back in to my chair.

Connor turned his collar up against the cold

24

November wind and rain, wrapping his arms around himself to hold the envelope, protectively, beneath his coat. It was good to be home, he had been gone too long. He pressed the button at the crossing and waited. The city had a fresh, vibrant feel. It had grown up in his absence, although — as in any beautiful garden — he knew if you lifted a stone there would still be a damp, dark place that was a hotbed for creepy crawlies who feared the light. For years, there hadn't been anyone to come back for — bar the odd cousin — the rest of his family were scattered across the globe, or they were dead.

Dead.

The familiar surge of pain behind his ribs bulged. He inhaled deeply, and blew out the grief. It caught him off guard sometimes. It was always there, in everything he did, but like a sensitive tooth that you became accustomed too, every now and then, something flicked the nerve, and the ache burned in him.

This visit was different. It was Michael's birthday — the first of his circle of old friends to turn forty — and they had celebrated well. Michael was a good mate and an invaluable support, particularly over recent months. He knew Connor needed a break and had set up a meeting with the publisher. Connor needed to stay focused; his writing had stopped him being washed away by the lapping waves of grief that had threatened his ability to go on. He looked up at the glass-fronted building and stepped into the warm, welcoming lobby of Ulster Press.

With Lucy at her Grandmother's, and Andrew out with a client, dinner for Jessica and I consisted mainly of fruit, and when I say fruit, I mean wine. We had wine for dinner. Continental meats, plump black olives, and juicy grapes were on hand to pick at while we put the world to rights.

"How come you were in the office today? I thought you were allergic to work on a Friday?" I asked Jessica, as I burst a fat olive between my tongue and the roof of my mouth.

"I had a meeting with the friend, of a friend, who has written 'the next best seller'. He was only available this afternoon," Jessica said, as she topped up my wine glass.

"Any good?"

"I have no idea. It'll go in the slush pile." Jessica flopped on to the sofa next to me, and ran her fingers through her hair. "We're so busy at the minute Cat, response times are terrible, and, by all accounts, this guy's had it hard. If it's going to be a 'thanks, but no thanks', it should be swift, at least."

"Want me to give it the once over?" I offered. "I'm heading up to Donegal tomorrow with nothing to do but relax."

"That would be fabulous," Jessica enthused. "He's not a writer as such, so I don't know what standard it will be, but the first four chapters are in an envelope in my briefcase. Now, tell me what has you frowning." Jessica tipped her head to one side, ready to listen.

"I feel like I've been drugged Jess," I explained,

26

"and it's left me with a craving for more. I'm even having hallucinations." I filled her in on my daydreams and visions of Mr Mystery.

"Half the population of Belfast has dark hair and blue eyes, Cat. Don't be too hard on yourself, but I do know what this is all about." She paused for effect, taking a long slug of her wine before meeting my questioning gaze. "You're ready," she declared triumphantly.

"For…?"

"For LOVE!" Jessica grinned and clasped her hands to her heart. "You are ready to love again."

"I might have expected some romantic clap trap from you." I threw a cushion at her as she rose to get more wine.

"It makes sense. You've always been adamant you didn't want to live with a man again, let alone get married. Maybe you just didn't want to be married to Jack, and with him gone for good, sorry,"—she placed a hand on my shoulder as she passed—"your inner Goddess has released you to look for a mate again, now there's no chance of you going back over."

I laughed at her expression; she was so pleased with herself. She was like an excited puppy when she got like this, and her enthusiasm was infectious.

"Okay,"—I mulled it over—"say you're right, my, what was it? 'Inner Goddess' has imprinted on some mystery man, a complete stranger, and one I am never likely to run into again. How is that helpful?"

"Serendipity!" Jessica exclaimed. The wine and talk of romance had given her a wistful, mushy smile.

"Who's she, and how does she know my man?" I asked with fake indignation.

"You remember the film? I made you sit through it a couple of years ago. You loved it, said 'It restored your faith in fate'."

I did remember. John Cusack and Kate Beckinsale, a magical film about two people who met and felt an instant connection. They relied on destiny to bring them together when the time was right. I grinned.

"So, you're saying what? I'll find him on the morning of his wedding?"

"I am saying I hold great faith in serendipity, and if you're meant to be together, fate will make it happen." Jessica clasped her hands together, and beamed at me.

I shook my head laughing. "You're so full of shit."

CHAPTER 5

Early Saturday morning I picked up supplies from Sainsbury's, loaded up the car, and headed west on the M1 from Belfast with food to last a week, enough wine for a party, and Paloma Faith to serenade me once the radio signal faded.

'Lucy's Cottage' was almost three hours away on the west coast of County Donegal, near Carrick. From the front, the building was single storey and slung low. Painted a soft sage green, it sank into the surroundings and didn't startle them, and topped with a grey slate roof. I opened the front door, to the left the kitchen rolled away with its cream walls, agar, and pottery loaded pine dresser, offering homely perfection. Through the small hallway, a spacious lounge opened out to the right. A large fireplace with wooden beam mantle dominated the room, its imposing stature softened by the lit church candles, and the fire crackling a welcome from within its belly. The sofa was plump and inviting, beckoning you to sink in to its arms, everything about this room called for you to relax.

The lounge spread into a dining area, before meeting the kitchen in a horseshoe, and the floor to ceiling glass panes offered a spectacular view across the rolling green garden to the cliff edge, and onwards to the ever-changing shades of the ocean, and the weather it brought to shore. It was as beautiful here in a storm as it was on a summer's day, more so perhaps. The drama and electrical tension of a rumbling thunderstorm was invigorating. I paused to take in its restorative quality. This area was part of an extension that made the rear of the cottage two storeys high. The en-suite bedrooms were on the ground floor, beneath the dining room, and not visible from the road.

I headed down the stairs to the master bedroom, French doors opened out to a decked patio, with its ostentatious hot tub and wicker furniture protected from the elements by a canopy and glass windbreaker. I threw open the doors and held my breath against the icy onslaught of salty air, as it whipped around me. Out in the garden autumn had arrived with a vengeance, and the burnt orange leaves hung limply on the cherry blossom, clashing vividly with the baby blue sky.

I adored this cottage, I was still awe struck that it was mine. It was a haven from the rest of the world, and I could relax, with no need to force sociable conversation, or feign interest in a client's ramblings. I was insular, not just tolerating my own company, but relishing it.

I spent the day in kitchen therapy, peeling, chopping, slicing, and the tension of the last few weeks unravelled as I hummed along to music. I rarely put the effort in at home, cooking for one was almost pointless when time was valuable, and I was never short of dinner invitations. Here in the cottage, time was a welcome companion, and I leisurely created vegetable soup, a big pot of chilli, popped a gammon joint in the slow cooker, and potatoes in the oven. This cook-in would feed me for a good couple of days.

With the kitchen cleaned, I dried my hands and flicked on the dishwasher. It was almost four. I poured a glass of wine, placating myself that holiday rules applied, and moved into the lounge, throwing a couple of logs on to the glowing embers. The fire stretched from its slumber, flicking its flaming arms around the fodder. My favourite DVD's were lined up on a bookshelf, and I ran a finger along their spines in deliberation. Working Girl, City of Angels, Cocktail, The Holiday. Yes, that would do nicely. Loading the disc into the player, I sunk into the comfort of the sofa, and curled my feet up. The warm buzz of a guaranteed happy ending was already forming inside me, and as the film unfolded, I wore a soppy, satisfied grin.

Once the evening had progressed to the point I was sure no rambler in their right mind would be out this far from civilisation, I headed downstairs and filled the hot tub. Out on the decking armed with a towel, wine, and the plastic wallet with the manuscript in, I set them down and shed my fluffy dressing gown.

The reflection of my tattoo in the bedroom mirror surprised me, as it often did. Its existence, not always visual, was often forgotten, the significance was not. A single stargazer lily, its tendrils sweeping from my side, down under my hip bone, surrounded by twenty tiny stars. One for each week I had carried him.

Jack had hated it, stating it was a reminder of our loss every time he seen me naked. I had long since reconciled I was as much to blame for Jack's affair as he was. It had been easy to blame him at first, but in losing our baby, I had shut down emotionally, and physically, I couldn't give him the affection he needed. The barmaid, with her youthful, unscarred heart, and promises of fertility, must have been a welcome oasis after the desert of our marriage.

I slipped into the warm, soothing water, the steam melted my thoughts until the past evaporated, and all that remained was peace. The ocean whispered its promises to the shore, and the moon cast a brilliant band of light through the black night on to the undulating expanse of water.

Confident my emotions were suitably cleansed; I dried my hands and unzipped the wallet. A waft of manliness escaped from the pages, reminding me of scented love letters from history. He smelt good; I liked him already.

How Will You Remember Me?

By

Max Walker

If you heard tomorrow
That I had died today,
Would your heart feel sorrow?
What would you think, or say?
Would you have a fleeting memory
Of a moment way back when?
Would you try to place me
As you knew me through a friend?
Would you recall an evening
When we laughed until we cried?
Were you always there for me
When I needed you at my side?
Could you say that you knew
What had meaning in my life?
Were you one of the few
Who never caused me strife?
So, how will you remember me?
If you do at all
Did you miss the opportunity
To make that one last call?
Do you think you'll miss me,
Or think of me again?
Will you replay a memory
That's just a dead end

CHAPTER ONE : THE END

October was unseasonably warm, and the heat of the hospice enforced the blue-sky view from the window. It was almost tropical, hot and humid.

I stood over the bed and tucked the duvet around his skeletal frame, smoothing down the cover. He looked so peaceful. Where had his morphine-cushioned subconscious taken him to find shelter from his pain? I was nauseous; not sure if it was the inevitable loss, expectant grief, or fear.

My life had taken me to situations others would only experience in their sweat-soaked nightmares. I had seen innocent children cut down inches from the safety of my hands, charged through hailstorms of enemy fire, collapsed into the safety of buildings, and thanked a God I didn't believe in. I had taken life. In combat, in the name of my country, and in defence of myself, and others.

Nothing had prepared me for this day, as I watched a man I had loved all my life — my hero — hang precariously between this life and the next.

"How's he doing mate?"

Tight-lipped, I shook my head at the occupant in the next bed.

"Not good Simon, they say it won't be long now. He's ready."

"Are you ready?" Simon asked.

I blew out the tension and rubbed my hands over my face.

"If he is, I am too," I answered, with honesty. "That's how it's always been, since we were kids. He forged the path and I followed."

"He's one of the lucky ones, he has no regrets. Not one." Simon sank back into his pillows. He looked older than his years, his hair was gone, face drawn, and exhausted, yellow-tinged body ravaged by cancer.

"Do you have regrets Simon?" I asked. I was curious, was dying without regrets any easier than dying with them?

"Only one. Here," he beckoned me, reaching for his wallet, pulling out a dog-eared photograph. "This is my regret, my first wife. She was the love of my life."

He strolled down his memory lane, recounting how they met as teenagers and forged a life together, a good and happy life, until his actions had pushed them apart. He didn't elaborate, but the echoes of emotion in his jaded eyes told me he hadn't behaved well, and he knew it.

"I need you to hang on to that photo." Simon

rubbed away the tears pooled in his hazel eyes. "It would not do to have the current missus find her predecessor in my wallet after all these years. We have been happy, and I have no desire to hurt her."

Simon was a man near the end of his time, and he gave the impression he had never had a conversation as emotionally charged as this. He was a man's man. His talk revolved around which horse was carrying his money, where his last job was, and what his chances were with the new nurse. I felt honoured he trusted me enough to open up, to use me as his confessional, in his dying days.

"I'll maybe get to meet her one day? I could give her this back?" I offered. The unspoken understanding that 'one day' would be Simon's funeral hung heavy in the air.

Simon smiled and squeezed my forearm. "I'd rest easy mate."

The nurse arrived, and the moment was broken. I placed Simon's picture safely in my pocket, and retreated to hold the hand of my dying brother.

How Will You Remember Me?

CHAPTER 6

I was hooked. The opening chapter concluded with the devastating loss of half of himself, the death of his identical twin. The story jumped back, starting with his earliest memories and their formative years. It detailed the protagonist's military background, and how he had faced the disapproval of his mother — an Irish Catholic woman — who fiercely held on to the beliefs of her father. Her son was fighting for a Queen who had torn her country apart.

He recounted how the army had pushed him beyond his limits and broken him, only to put its arms around him and bring him into the fold. It was his friend, his family, his life. He described a tour of the former Yugoslavia's civil war, and he eloquently drew similarities to the sectarian troubles of his homeland.

He painted heart-wrenching scenes with beautiful, sensitive words, which were hard to reconcile with the tough, masculine soldier image his outer shell portrayed. He talked of death and dying, and of killing, with the emotional distance needed to survive these experiences.

The four chapters had me gripped, and the synopsis went on to describe how a cheating girlfriend had emotionally destroyed him, and threw himself into his work to save what sanity he had left. He left the army and worked as a mercenary, offering personal protection to the wealthy elite and their families, earning obscene amounts of money he couldn't spend working 24/7. A victim of his own success. I felt an immediate connection; his self-preservation strategy was familiar. I knew, instinctively, this was autobiographical, the realism and emotion on each page was not a product of imagination. It had been lived.

I lifted my head and winced at the pain in my neck. I hadn't moved in hours. I lifted a wrinkled toe out of the water, and saw it was time to get out of the tub. Wrapped in the welcome warmth of my dressing gown, I gathered my things, and pulled the French doors closed behind me, pushing my feet into waiting slippers and bounded up the stairs. I stoked and fed the sleepy fire, grabbed my iPhone and found the email address on the front of the manuscript.

To : MaxWalker@gmail.com

Subject : Manuscript – How Will You Remember Me?

Dear Max,

With reference to the above, I am reviewing your submission on behalf of Ulster Press.

Please email the completed manuscript to me at your earliest convenience.

Regards,

Catherine

Sent from my iPhone

I kept the email brief. I wanted to tell him how I identified with so much of his writing, how sorry I was at the loss of his brother, how excited I was by his words, but I had seen submissions before that died after the first few chapters, so I held back, and decided on an early night.

I'm in the hot tub. The steam rises in wisps around me. I am warm, content. My eyes search the green expanse towards the point it disappears over the cliff.

I feel him before I see him. Goosebumps ripple up my arms and my stomach tightens as I catch the scent of him. There he is, striding towards me. A khaki t-shirt stretches across his broad shoulders and curved chest. I raise a hand to shade my eyes, hungrily watching his every move.

My anticipation builds. He is as I remember. Tall,

handsome, with dark hair, and sparkling blue eyes. I am naked in front of this stranger, yet I am unconcerned. He peels off his t-shirt, and unbuttons his camouflage pants. They drop low, displaying moulded obliques and…

I was in darkness, momentarily confused by my surroundings as my wakened state harmonised with the hot tub floozy of my dreams. My heart raced and the muscles clenching low in my stomach gave testament to how real the dream was. Throwing back the duvet, I padded to the bathroom and switched on the light. I held a flannel under a gush of icy water, and squeezed out the excess, pressing it to my face and neck.

"Tramp," I scolded my flushed reflection, and switched off the light, before returning to a fitful sleep.

The vibration of the mobile, on the wooden bedside table, announced the arrival of an email, and stirred me from my slumber. The soft morning light beamed through the window, and outside the day was dry and crisp. I stretched, reaching for the phone.

From : Maxwalker@gmail.com

To : CatherineHarvey@CHP.com

Subject : Manuscript – How Will You Remember Me?

Dear Catherine,

Please find attached the completed manuscript as

requested. May I take this opportunity to thank you, for your time and speedy response; I had been warned it may take months to hear anything at all.

I'll offer an apology now, as you will have gathered I am not a writer, but I had a story to tell.

If you have any queries please do not hesitate to contact me

Warmly,

Max

1 Attachment

Sent from my iPhone

From : CatherineHarvey@CHP.com

To : Maxwalker@gmail.com

Subject : Manuscript – How Will You Remember Me?

Hi Max

Thanks. One query, is this autobiographical?

Regards

Catherine

Sent from my iPhone

I peeled myself away from the exquisite comfort of my bed, and headed for the shower. Stepping under the powerful stream of water, I washed away the sleepy remnants of the night. Refreshed and wrapped in a soft bath towel, I picked up my phone.

From : Maxwalker@gmail.com

To : CatherineHarvey@CHP.com

Subject : Manuscript – How Will You Remember Me?

Hi Catherine

Yes, my brother died recently. I wrote the bulk of the manuscript at his bedside over the last few months of his life; the beginning written at the end, if that makes sense. I had little else to do and, in many ways, revisiting my life so far, and seeing the previous events I had overcome, gave me the strength to cope when this battle was lost

Thanks again,

Max

I felt a flash of his grief in my stomach, in awe of his cathartic journey, travelled at the bedside of his dying brother.

From : CatherineHarvey@CHP.com

To : Maxwalker@gmail.com

Subject : Manuscript – How Will You Remember Me?

Hi Max

I am sorry for your loss, and cannot begin to imagine how you are feeling. Please accept my deepest condolences.

I will review the rest of the manuscript, and Ulster Press will be in touch in due course.

Take Care,

Catherine

Sent from my iPhone

I dressed and spent half an hour in the kitchen, setting up the coffee machine, and warming a couple of croissants. I spooned out some fresh fruit salad, and picked at it as I fired up the iPad and saved down the manuscript. I poured the coffee and set it on the breakfast bar with the warmed pastries, which were now sliced and filled with melting butter and sweet strawberry jam.

Although I was desperate to return to Max's life, I stuck to the disciplined routine of checking emails, my calendar, and social media accounts. I viewed the local news feeds, and checked the weather forecast. A text dropped in; 'Speed-dial Steve'— would his services be required, before he made plans he couldn't break? I was tempted, frustrated from my dream which replayed in my mind with unnerving clarity. I let him down gently, telling him I was in hormonal seclusion and he was best at a distance. Half true any way. Besides, sleeping with Steve would be like cheating on Mr Mystery. Sometimes, I amazed myself, not always in a good way.

I refilled my cup, lifted the iPad, sank in to the welcoming comfort of the sofa, and took up my position in Max's memories.

The rest of his army career detailed tours in Germany, Cyprus, and Canada, telling stories of scrapes with the lads, and of a stray dog who befriended him. His military career was woven with humour, adventure, and heartbreak, and made fascinating reading. His writing style was personal, as if he were talking to you over a drink. Max told a good story, and his exploits reminded me of a much-loved friend back home, who had often told me tales of his colourful army life.

My stomach growled when it passed lunchtime. I piled gammon, pickles, olives, and some crusty bread on to a plate, grabbed a bottle of water from the fridge, and returned to the Catherine-shaped depression in the sofa.

I befriended Max through his stories, I knew him from reading his thoughts, his reactions, and I liked him. He wasn't perfect, far from it, but he was very human, and so when he described his emotional destruction at the hands of a cheating girlfriend, I understood the pain.

Leaving the army, he took the well-travelled path into personal security, after a formed soldier in Oman threw him a lifeline. Working as a mercenary, he was embroiled in more trials and tribulations, still relayed with the same mix of humour and tension.

Evening drew in around the cottage. The cold night nipped at my stillness, and I built a fire. The toughest decision of the day was whether to have soup or chilli for dinner. I went for the chilli; it would warm me until the fire took hold. I filled a bowl, surrounded it with tortilla chips, and sat at the breakfast table to continue reading.

When Max received word his brother was sick, he returned to the UK, initially as a prospective bone marrow donor, and had been his companion and carer for almost a year. There was less humour in the final chapters, and a story of romance and regret pulled at the heartstrings in the final pages.

I would live twice the life from here on. Once for me, and again for my brother. I would continue his charitable work, in his name, and we would go home to Belfast, building a future to fulfil his wishes. Together, even if the other half of me was in an urn.

I will remember you always. My brother, my friend, my hero.

It was almost midnight when I finished, feeling as if I had stepped off a rollercoaster, breathless and dizzy. Drained, yet restless, the last of the adrenaline disbursed. It was too late to call Jessica.

From : CatherineHarvey@CHP.com

To : Jessica@UlsterPress.co.uk

Subject : Max Walker – How Will You Remember Me?

Hi Honey,

Re the above - sign him. Today.

Speak soon, Love you

Cat xx

I had a good feeling about this manuscript, and about Max. My instincts were always spot-on with the reviews for Jessica, and of all the novels I had taken off the slush pile this one fired me up more than any other. I was exhausted and debated pulling the throw from the back of the sofa and sleeping where I sat, but knew I would regret it in the morning.

I cleared my pots, lifted a glass and decanted a generous measure of Port. I stopped to look passed the dining room's reflection in the windowpane, to the dark abyss beyond. Partially hidden, the moon silver-plated the clouds. The stars were visible through the cracks, glistening like a million diamonds, and the moonlight bounced off the sea. Sleepy, and warmed from the alcohol, I descended to my room and pulled the curtains to keep the morning light out as long as possible. Right now, I could sleep for a week; my body was heavy. I washed my face, cleaned my teeth, and crawled into bed.

I look up. I am outside, on the decking, confused how I got here, but not surprised I'm naked. He is here again. I smell him, and feel his heat behind me. I turn. He is shirtless; his combats hang low on his hips. I trace my finger across his chest and down his hard abdomen and…

I sat bolt upright. The dream washed over me, and I sank back into the pillows. This was not healthy. I didn't even know what 'this' was, but I knew it wasn't healthy. My scalp tingled, the idea he was thinking about me brushed my conscious thoughts.

"I need therapy," I muttered into the darkness.

He is here again. He stands in the garden where he spent his summers as a child, but he is grown now. The sun is warm on his exposed chest, but the wind bites into him, lashing with its fierce tongue. She hasn't seen him, and he takes in every inch of her naked beauty. Her blonde hair cascades down the centre of her smooth back. He stands behind her and she turns at his presence. He smiles as she draws a line across his chest, the heat from her gentle touch burns in him. He wants her.

The image had gone. His eyes were open, unseeing in the dark night. He never dreamed, ever, and now twice in as many nights he had seen her in his sleep.

How Will You Remember Me?

CHAPTER 7

Monday brought rain and high winds, not the drama of a thunderstorm, but enough to bring me to the dining room table to eat my breakfast and take in the view. The sky was extraordinary. The rolling clouds covered a spectrum from inky black to sparkling white, with every shade of grey between, but the strangest thing was the ribbons of orange light coursing through them, giving an eerie science-fiction feel.

The ocean was black, splintered by the crests of surging waves as they hurtled to shore, crashing and exploding against any obstacle in their path. The sea-spray arced high in to the air as the tide met the submerged rocks off the edge of the natural pier. There was so much energy out there it tired me just watching. Everything moved. The clouds, the sea, the spray, I was mesmerised by it and almost a little seasick. I pulled away and cleared my breakfast pots into the kitchen.

Despite the weather, I needed air. After spending yesterday reading, I was stiff and wanted to stretch my legs. I didn't go far, staying within sight of the cottage, I walked along the edge of the cliff. Not too near, but close enough to smell the sea and taste the salty spray on each blast of wind.

I felt so alive. The power of the sea and the bracing wind was invigorating, all thoughts of mystery men and therapy blown away. I felt cleansed, fresh, and dynamic. My past was no longer a burden, and the possibility of a future with someone who was more than a friend, or a convenient itch-scratcher, didn't seem as unbelievable as it had only a month ago.

My inner voice chattered excitedly, it often betrayed me. Christmas was looming on the horizon and there would be parties and events galore where I could meet a suitor. I halted my manic striding and pulled a face.

"Suitor? What am I, ninety?"

I laughed and skipped, yes skipped, back to the cottage with an unbridled enthusiasm that was unfamiliar, but felt amazing.

With one hand wrapped around a cup of hot soup, I pulled up my calendar and viewed the engagements already in the diary for December, checking them for potential. Nothing jumped out. These were regular events I attended year in year out with the same faces at each. Surely, if anyone suitable went I would have found him by now. I was a little disheartened; maybe this wasn't going to be as easy I first hoped.

I needed to attack this like a project. As always, I started with a mind-map, pulling all the pertinent details in a visual drawing. I wrote, in the centre of the note pad, OPERATION SOULMATE and circled it boldly; giggling at the level of pathetic I had reached. It was almost tongue-in-cheek, but I was happy to laugh at myself and even blush at the thought of anyone knowing I was doing it. I underlined the PURPOSE, with its direction arrow, was to FIND A PARTNER. Next was the CHARACTERISTICS I wanted, and, after circling the header, I made short strokes to mark out my criteria for a mate:

- Dark hair

- Blue eyes

- Tall

- Broad shouldered

- Caring

- Sensitive

- Masculine

- Humble

- Good humoured

- Confident

- Charitable

- Independent

Next was LOCATION, LOCATION, LOCATION. Where was I to meet this handsome, perfectly balanced human to sweep me off my feet? I made several lines:

- Parties

- Fundraisers

- Book launches

Where else? I tapped the pencil on my chin, deep in thought. I was missing a trick here, I didn't have time for hobbies but there must be another avenue. My attention drifted to the row of DVD's and one jumped out at me; '50 First Dates'. Of course! That was it; I needed some first dates. I needed to sign up for internet dating.

I fired up Google and typed in 'Belfast Dating'. Ten and a half million results, that was promising. The first link advised me the oceans were plentiful, and to dive in was free. All I needed was a duck-pout profile picture and a slutty tagline, and I would be awash with chavtastic sea creatures. I backed out of that one, as tempting as it sounded…

The next promised to find my perfect match, for a princely joining fee. The advert showed a loved-up couple, gazing at each other, arm in arm on a beach stroll. All that was missing was cupid's arrow and matching cardigans. I was a dating snob. Worse than that, I was a cynical dating snob.

The next link looked more interesting, an article about a woman who had returned to her native Belfast when her marriage collapsed. She found her old friends settled with children, and in the absence of a social network and accessible dating scene, she set up her own 'Singles Supper Club' and the concept was born. She now ran a successful company, vetting each new member, and hosting regular dinners in and around the city, with numerous success stories. This sounded familiar. I typed in the search bar 'Singles Supper Club Belfast'. This was the trading name of PM Introductions Limited. Of course, Paula McCullagh was a client. I pulled out my mobile and searched the contacts list, no time like the present. The call rang twice.

"Hello, you have reached the voicemail of Paula McCullagh, please leave a message and I will get back to you as soon as possible, for details of our next meet please see the company website."

"Paula, this is Catherine Harvey, can you give me a call when you're free? Thank you."

Another online service had caught my eye, advertising its suitability for 'business professionals in Northern Ireland looking for friends, fun, and maybe more'. I wasn't sure what was implied by the 'and maybe more', but it looked classier than the oceanic offerings earlier, so I set about completing the form and paying my joining fee. Nothing ventured, nothing gained.

Next of interest was the 'Titanic Experience's New Year's Eve Masquerade Ball'. I liked the look of that. It was marked in my calendar; I sent the acceptance to Lisa. I was invited to so many events, anything we were involved in had a representative from CHP attend.

The Masquerade Ball was a charity fundraising event for a local suicide prevention group, which we were pleased to support. Not a week went by without some youngster, often several, giving up on life. Suicide was such a permanent solution to what were often temporary problems, and, particularly on the outskirts of the city, it was seen as the way out. I thought of how Max's brother, and Jack, had ferociously fought for their lives when others threw it away. I didn't judge them, they believed it was the only way, but I felt desperately sad for them, and those they left behind.

With my planner open, I noticed Lisa had booked in the stint at the soup kitchen. It was a company ritual. The Friday before Christmas, we would volunteer at the soup kitchen in the city centre before heading out for our celebrations. It was a humbling experience and made us all the more grateful for what we had to celebrate. Our jobs, our homes, our health, our family and friends, and each of us took a gift to leave under the tree. I accepted the invite and sent an email asking Lisa to remind everyone gifts needed to be practical; toiletries, thermals, socks - all welcomed by those living rough, or under the poverty line.

The night had closed in around the cottage and I flicked on the heating, too lazy to light a fire. I poured a large glass of wine, lifted my phone from the worktop and dropped a quick text to Jessica.

'What would you say if I told you I'd signed up for on-line dating? Xx'

The reply came through instantaneously.

'I'd say 'who is this and what have you done with

Catherine??' Haha Proud of you honey, we'll make a balanced human of you yet xx'

I picked another Rom-Com from the row of films, I was going soft, but I liked how it felt.

And so the week meandered by. I cooked, walked on the wind swept beach, and took the time to lift shells embedded in the damp sand. I gathered leaves and driftwood, and made a little fire in the garden, to mark Bonfire night on the English date, and not in July as they did here in Northern Ireland. I ate hotdogs and jacket potatoes, as we had as children, and greedily inhaled the smoky-scent of my clothes when I removed them later. This was one scent that invoked memories of my mother and Grandparents, a memory, blurred by time, of a bonfire at my Granddad's allotment. Sparklers, fireworks, and laughter.

There was always laughter in those early recollections. I remembered vividly my Nana sitting with me on her knee, explaining the significance of Remembrance Sunday.

'On the eleventh hour, of the eleventh day of the eleventh month, we will remember them'.

She told me the story of her evacuation to the country when she was no more than the age I was then, maybe six or seven. Taken from her home, but she had loved her farm family, and told tales of a life so different to her every day. She was almost sorry to return to her parents when the war ended, and had kept in touch with her other family all her life. Wearing a poppy in Belfast was often judged as sectarian, but I bought mine and wore it with pride, in honour of those that died in service, and as a tribute to my Nana. A woman of immense strength and influence in my life who had cared for me long after my parents had died, and whom I had missed every day since her death ten years earlier. If she had been alive, I wouldn't have moved to Belfast, I simply could not have left her.

Sunday afternoon arrived again too soon. The sky had wrung out every drop of water it held and the clouds had scurried away, redundant. The watery sun hung low across the horizon, bouncing its rays off the rain-drenched roads. I packed the last of my things into the car and closed the boot, bade a mental farewell to the cottage and pulled away, promising I would return soon. I pushed a CD into the player, cranked it up and sang along.

My heart felt light and carefree. Life was looking good and anything was possible. Buoyed up by the opportunities opening up now I had accepted I was ready to share my life with someone, I grinned. Even thinking that made my cynical inner goddess roll her eyes, but it was exciting.

I reached for my sunglasses and lowered the visor. The evening sun glinted in the rear view mirror, distracting me with its powerful glare. I was glad I was heading east, away from the blinding sun. I wasn't far from home as I slowed to take the bend, over the crest of the hill, down towards the sprawling city of Belfast.

CHAPTER 8

Connor landed in Belfast, having tied up loose ends in England, and collected a rental car from the airport. It would do for now. In a couple of days he would pick up the keys for his new home, and to kill time he had decided to head west to Donegal, the playground of his youth. It had called to him in his dreams of late, reminding him of happier times.

And of her.

He was frustrated, not only by the heat of his dreams, but because she was faceless. He remembered the gold in her hair, the curve of her breast, her presence, but her features were blurred.

The traffic was light as he began his ascent out of the city. Ahead, a car pulled across the warning lines in the middle of the road, around a slow climbing lorry. Connor shook his head. That dickhead would be blinded by the setting sun as he hit the crest of the hill.

The Black X5 broke over the horizon and was confronted by the Passat, powering towards it. The BMW veered sharply to its left. The front wings collided, the innocent vehicle violently whipped back on itself. The rogue car accelerated away. The lorry's airbrakes screamed a protest. Connor stopped his car, flicked on the hazard lights, and popped the boot. He threw down the warning sign into the road and lifted the first aid kit. Pulling his mobile from his pocket, he punched in 999, and ran to the hissing vehicle. He relayed details of the accident location to the call handler, signalled to the truck driver to halt any oncoming traffic, and circled the damaged car.

Fluid streamed from under the engine block. Petrol. He paused. No smoke, little fire risk. He checked for passengers inside the vehicle and for any thrown clear on impact. One occupant. Female, unconscious. Her head slumped towards her left shoulder. The driver's door window was smashed. Her face was swelling from the impact, half of it looked like a Halloween mask. It was superficial, but she had hit the glass with some force to smash it. She would have a fracture or two, possibly whiplash, and a hell of a headache.

He opened the car door, killed the engine, and placed his cheek in front of her nose and mouth to feel for breath, watching her chest rise and fall for the count of ten. She was breathing evenly, no wheezing. Her airways were clear and nothing was punctured.

He took a clean pad from the first aid kit.

"Hello?"

No response.

"Are you okay? What's your name?"

Nothing.

"Can you hear me?"

Again.

"Can you hear me?"

Her eyes flickered. Enthused, Connor called once more, "What's your name?"

He monitored her pulse, and her breathing, watching for signs of shock, ticking off a mental checklist. Connor held a dressing against the streaming head wound, the blood pasted her once blonde hair across her face. He pulled a foil blanket from its packet and laid it over her, all the while talking, telling her what he was doing, and watching for a response.

As he worked, Connor profiled the driver. Approximately 5'7", 130-140lbs, her clothes were casual, but well made, her handbag boasted a designer label. He scanned the car. She was unmarried, no wedding ring and no indent or tan line. Childless, no car seat.

He heard the ambulance approaching before he saw it. Connor gave his assessment of the scene, the driver, and her condition, and stepped away to let the paramedics take control. He waved a hand in thanks to the truck driver and returned to his car to wait for the police.

Adrenaline pulsed through him. It felt good to see action; he had missed it.

"Can you hear me?"

'Yes'

"What's your name?"

'Catherine, Catherine Harvey.'

The words formed in my head, but the fog trapped them. My hearing was muffled, my body weightless, yet heavy. The voice penetrated the confusion, repeating questions, and giving a commentary on what he was doing. The tone was strong, calm, and commanding, but the accent soft, local. I tried to open my eyes. Pain shot from my head, down through my neck and shoulder, and nausea washed over me. The starry blackness spun. I sank into oblivion.

Disinfectant. The iodine-scented hospital type.

Jessica. She was upset, I could tell by the tone of her voice. I tried to turn to the sound of her voice.

Oh sweet Jesus, my head.

What had I been drinking? A wave of pain washed away my conscious thought.

"How is she?" there was concern in this male voice. I recognised it. I frowned. Ah, that hurt.

"She's still sleeping. She took a nasty knock. It

might take some time for her to come around."

Who was Jessica talking to? Who was she talking about? I fought to surface through the cloying fogginess in my brain. I was too nosey, I wanted in on the conversation. A gentle kiss tickled my left cheek and I turned towards it.

"Catherine?" The man's voice was urgent. "Cath, can you hear me?"

I fought to open my eyes, the left complied but the right was glued shut. The voice belonged to Speed-dial Steve. Why was he here? Oh no, had I made a drunken call to him and passed out?

"What happened?" I whispered. The stark white walls were harsh on my eye. "Where am I?"

Jessica appeared at Steve's side.

"It's okay honey. You were in a wee accident and bumped your head, nothing to worry about." Jessica's words were calmer than her voice portrayed. "You've a black eye and a few stitches, but you're still gorgeous, isn't she Steve?"

"Beautiful," he affirmed, concern etched around his grey-green eyes. He kissed me again. "Thank God you're okay."

"I'm tired." I tried to smile. "Oh that's sore!" I raised my hand to my face, gingerly touching around my swollen eye and patched up head. "Jess, could you help me get cleaned up?"

"You need to rest a while yet; nurse has to check you over before you're allowed out of bed." She stroked my hair from the good side of my face. "I'll sort you out later, try and sleep some more."

At times, Jessica was more like my mother than my best friend, and it felt good. I nodded and closed my eyes, slipping into the comfortable blackness.

One night in hospital was more than enough for anyone, how they expected anyone to get well with the constant disturbances — and prods and pokes — was beyond me. I settled back in the flat, with Jessica fussing around.

"I can stay tonight, but Andrew's away tomorrow, with work, and I don't want to bring Lucy over yet"—she bit her lip and looked a little guilty—"I think you'd scare her, no offence."

"Oh none taken!" I giggled. "These painkillers are great." I knew my head hurt, but I just didn't care.

She tucked the quilt around me. "Steve said he might pop by tomorrow." She was pottering around the bedroom, unpacking from my stay at the cottage. It seemed so long ago.

"Mr Friday? On a Tuesday? Whatever next?" I sobered a little. "He knows he's out of luck though, right?"

"Have you seen the state of your bake? Again, no offence."

She ducked as I threw the book from my bedside table at her.

"You read the leaflet," I laughed. "Head injuries can cause mood swings. I can't be held responsible."

"So, what was your excuse before?" She asked. I slapped playfully at her as she flopped onto the bed. "You gave me a fright, I can't think about what could have happened." She hugged my good side. "At least they caught up with the driver. The Police called earlier, the guy at the scene got the registration number."

"That's good. I remember someone talking to me, was that a paramedic?"

"No, some guy who stopped to help, he looked after you until the ambulance got there."

The random act of kindness touched me. These days too many people would walk by, it would be good to thank him. I closed my eyes, drained by the conversation, thoughts washed away on a wave of exhaustion and codeine. The familiar blackness cocooned me.

I spent the week moving from bed, to the sofa, and back. Everything was such an effort, a combination of the accident and the painkillers. The swelling was going down, the bruise had faded from a deep purple to a greeny-yellow, and Lucy had visited. Having insisted she was brave enough, she cried at the sight of me, but not because she was frightened, because I was hurt.

The flat overflowed with flowers, gifts, and cards, as word had spread among friends and clients. Jessica had fielded any attempts to visit, and I was grateful for it. I was lucky, not just surviving the accident, minimal injuries, but to have someone to look after me. She shopped, cooked, and cared for me, staying over to keep me company when she could.

The strangest development of the week had been Steve. Shaken by my accident, he wanted to try traditional dating once I was back on my feet. In my codeine-induced state of fluffiness, I had agreed, but I wasn't sure such a radical shift in our relationship would be tenable, although I was willing to try it. I owed him that.

Our first date was supposed to be something simple, dinner and drinks in a seafood restaurant in the city. It was one of my favourite places to eat, the black and white exterior was clean and sharp, its name blazing in gold letters.

We sat under the leaded window, the streetlight glowing through the stained glass and sipped at a Sauvignon Blanc. The dining room was completely unpretentious, dress was casual, the furniture rustic and comfortable. Just perfect, I had been looking forward to it all week.

Chat came easy; there were no edges on our friendship. What we had was fun, experimental, satisfying, but it was just sex. I had never wanted any emotional attachment; you got hurt when feelings were involved. This way was cleaner, simpler. Safer.

Later, Steve sat across from me, fiddling with his floppy, dark-brown hair, pushing his food around his plate, his face strained, almost frowning. His fingers drummed rhythmically on the wooden table. He was putting me off my food, which was hard to do. I put my fork down, took a drink, and went for it.

"Steve, what is it?" I asked.

"I think I love you."

Oh shit.

How Will You Remember Me?

CHAPTER 9

"He said what?" Jessica spun around to face me. "I knew something was wrong with him, but I thought he was worried about losing his easy touch"—I opened my mouth to protest—"no offence!" she said, setting a plate in front of me. She sat opposite me across the kitchen table, and poured the wine. Her Sunday lunches were legendary, and even though it was only the two of us she had still made the effort.

I laughed. "That will be in your obituary 'She meant no offence'. Jess it was awful, I know he has seen parts of me I couldn't see without a mirror, but, technically, it was our first — and last — date, and he was telling me he loved me. Just wrong."

"So, what did you do?" Jessica asked.

"I did what any sensitive, wise woman of the world would do in that situation." She raised a quizzical eyebrow at me. "I got drunk."

Later that evening, back at the flat, I snuggled into a chocolate leather oversized chair, and looked out across the lough. I was content; well fed and watered by Jessica. The view from here brought me peace, it was the reason I bought the place. At dusk, the lights across the city sparkled; signalling life and vitality, as they spread up the hills that curved around the city like a protective wall. A couple of tethered boats bobbed about in the marina, bunting tickled by the onshore breeze, and the Odyssey entertainment complex rose up behind them.

On to the right, following the rise out of the city, I saw headlights coming over the crest of a hill. Their beams signalled the exact point I had crashed. I shivered.

Belfast Castle nestled into the side of the Cave Hill, glowing majestically, bathed in warm light. Completed by the Marquis of Donegall in 1870, it was donated to the city by his descendants. It was a magnificent structure designed by Charles Lanyon and his son in a Scottish baronial style, and boasted fabulous gardens, and incredible views over Belfast, the lough, and beyond. It was a gloriously romantic venue, if I ever got married it would be there; how many people got married in a castle? I grinned; I was developing some kind of romantic illness, 'Cinderella Syndrome'. I had the castle lined up; I just needed to find a prince. I shook my head, if Jessica could read my thoughts she would be clapping her hands in glee.

Across the water from the castle rose the impressive structure housing the Titanic Experience. Based on the hull of the ill-fated ship, the silver building rose from the slipways that launched the Titanic, unfinished, the heaviest object ever moved by man at that time. The project was an incredible feat of engineering by Harland & Wolff. The visitor centre opened in April 2012 to commemorate the centenary of its maiden voyage. I had heard it questioned many times, as to why the city celebrated the building of Titanic with such pride when the unsinkable ship sank on its first outing. Blood, sweat, and tears went into the world's finest liner and, as locals would say, 'She was all right when she left here…'

The skyline was heavy with purple-grey clouds, broken to display patches of ice-blue sky still illuminated by the setting sun. I wished I could paint, to capture the unique mix of deep violet and slate grey; a photograph would never do it justice. The rippling lough reflected the mesmerising palette of colours. I loved living by the water, even the gentlest lapping had a restorative quality, and in warmer weather, I sat on the balcony and let it wash away the stresses of the day.

Lough side, at the front of the apartments, couples strolled arm in arm, talking, admiring the view, and a sculpture of the Titanic festooned with brilliant blue lights. Children ran around their parents, bounding up and down the steps, and climbing on the over-sized wooden benches.

At the water's edge stood a lone figure. A man, tall

with broad shoulders, his features hidden in the dusky shadows, head bowed. A healthy curiosity, and vivid imagination, piqued my interest, and I moved closer to the window. What was he doing? Was he thinking, or praying? He looked as if he might be. He had folded his arms in front of him. Did he have something in his arms? I couldn't make it out, a combination of failing eyesight and fading sunlight. His shoulders were slumped forward, and as he bent down and lent through the railings, for a moment, I thought he was going to disappear into the inky blackness. He straightened up, and raised his hand. A greeting, an acknowledgement, or farewell maybe? Slowly, he walked away and, inexplicably, I felt sad.

Connor walked along the pathway, towards the illuminated sculpture of Titanic, and stopped at the water's edge. People meandered about in conversation, oblivious to him, and what he held in his arms. The sky was spectacular; it was a gift. A birthday gift. Connor dropped his head and, silently, talked to an unseen confidante.

'How's it going? I miss you man, but I'm carrying on, as I said I would. It's hard, so it is, but Michael's helping, and he's got me in to see your woman, the publisher.' He pushed his fingers into the corners of his eyes as tears pooled there. 'I'm not sure how I've got through this day, mate. Another first, a birthday without you. A new world of hurt.'

Connor leant through the railings, and unscrewed the urn lid. He tipped the ashes onto the damp air, and watched as they sank into the sombre water. He straightened up and raised a hand skywards.

"Happy Birthday mate."

How Will You Remember Me?

CHAPTER 10

Friday came quickly. The switch on of the Christmas lights, and the arrival of the fabulous Continental market in the grounds of City Hall, marked the start of the yuletide season. Lucy burst into my office brimming with excitement, closely followed by Jessica. She gripped me in a bear hug, before stepping back to inspect me, brow furrowed. I stared back, straight faced, as she peered at me.

"Your eye is still a bit purple, but it's getting better, and your fringe is hiding your cut," She surmised. "That's good, but you're pale and a bit skinny."

"Don't you worry about me sweetie," I reassured her, "with all those glorious food stalls outside for a month, I won't be skinny for long."

We gathered around the conference table. Jessica handed me a take-out coffee, and opened a box of white chocolate and cranberry cookies she had brought with her. Outside the window, City Hall loomed impressively before us, bathed in an ethereal golden aurora. Ice-white fairy lights glinted among the leafless trees in the grounds, and the log cabin stalls of the market formed a festive village, welcoming visitors to the fold.

People choked Royal Avenue, as far as the eye could see. Men and women of all ages, many with young children on their shoulders, strained to see Peppa Pig flick the switch and announce the arrival of Christmas. Even from our vantage point, high above the crowds, the atmosphere was electric. Anticipation was building, for not only the lighting ceremony, but also the season and all it promised.

I loved Christmas, and had never understood the 'bah-humbug'ers. Even at the most desperate times in my life, the excitement, and hope, of Christmas offered a life-line, a promise all was not lost, and of better times to come. Sure, I had always spent it with people I loved, my parents, grandparents, sister, husband, and in recent years good friends. Nothing gave me greater pleasure than shopping for the perfect gift, and the thrill at a loved one's delight on receiving it. I never wanted anything for Christmas, for me it was all about the giving.

The anticipation I had felt before the accident was beginning to return, anything was possible. I was with two of my favourite people in the world, in a place I adored, successful and self-sufficient. I had worked hard and, some would say, paid a high price, nearing forty with no significant other or children, but I still felt blessed. I had a life I loved, and was ready to share it.

We went down as the crowds eased, and melted in to the river of people that oozed around the market stalls. As a lover of smells, this was my nirvana. The charcoal scorched meats, sweet toasted waffles and syrup, freshly ground coffee, hot chocolate, the earthy tinge of spilt beer and warm punter, and at this time of year the ever-present aroma of cinnamon.

Lucy gripped my hand. "Where are we going to first?" Her eyes were bright with adventure, a pink, fur-trimmed hat framed her rosy cheeks, and the cold air snatched away her words in white puffs. A rush of affection caught in my throat.

"What do you think? Foot-long Frankfurters or fudge? It's your call." I wasn't sure who was more excited, her or me.

"Fudge!" she yelled, pulling Jessica and me in search of the infamous sweet stall to fulfil all our sugar-based desires.

Milling around the staged Christmas village I recognised faces, some I waved at, and others I hugged, allaying concerns for my welfare. I assured them I was on the mend, and would catch up with them at this event, or that.

When the lure of my bed and its clean sheets was becoming unbearable, Paula McCullagh — the queen of Singledom — was elbowing her way through the throng, propelling herself in my direction. Paula was older than her dress sense suggested, and a fan of fake tan, hair extensions, and blood-red nails. She openly hunted the younger guy — a pure bred Cougar — and although an unsuspecting man would be powerless against her assertive pursuit, he would never regret the experience.

"Catherine!" She kissed the air either side of my face, and pulled me close. "I got your message"—her eyes flicked to Jessica—"are you okay to talk?"

"Oh yes, she knows all about my advances in to normality."

Jessica introduced herself, and Paula raised a perfectly drawn eyebrow. "Jessica, it's a pleasure." More air kisses. I grinned. Paula was Jessica's worst nightmare. "How is your gorgeous husband?" Paula scoured around us, touching her hair and licking her lips. "Is he with you?"

"No, he's at home, waiting for me." Jessica was riled. I was amused.

"Have you met Andrew, Paula?" I dripped innocence, as Jessica's weight transferred to my little toe.

"Sadly, no, but I'm a huge fan. I followed him in his rugby days, such an amazing player. So talented, so keen, so fit!" She cleared her throat, checking her enthusiasm. "He was a credit to the game, and it would be a genuine pleasure to meet him." She giggled and flashed her best smile at Jessica. "Will you be joining our next dinner, Catherine?"

"Sure, everything I've heard is positive," I said. "When and where?"

"First Saturday of every month, I'll drop you an

email with the time and place." She hugged me again. "It's good to see you on your feet. Jessica, lovely to meet you." The dazzling smile again that, knowing Jessica, she would read as 'I want your husband for breakfast'.

We watched her wiggle away, hand high in the air.

"Who was that lady?" Lucy asked, her eyes wide.

'Lady?' Jessica mouthed to me. "She's a client of Aunty Catherine's."

"And do you make sure everyone knows she's happening," Lucy asked, "or do you launch her?"

"Trust me Lucy, a lady like that does not require my assistance to launch." Jessica giggled at me. "Come on Missy, I'm ready for my bed."

"You sure you don't mind keeping her Cat?" Jessica asked, as she kissed Lucy goodbye.

"Not at all, give Andrew my love and enjoy your dinner"—I hugged her—"and we'll see you tomorrow, text me when you're up."

Lucy chattered non-stop, fired up on a heady mix of sugar and the promise of more fun back at the flat. After far too much ice-cream laden with hot fudgy sauce, she wrote her Christmas list, and picked gifts for her parents; a beautiful cream pashmina for her mummy, and an Ulster Rugby onesie for her daddy. Finally bathed, in her pyjamas, and tucked up in 'her' bedroom, she snuggled Niall, the One Direction-themed Build-a-Bear who had a beating heart and a foot that smelt like bubble-gum. I sat on the bed and

79

stroked her hair. Her eyes grew heavy; she fell asleep with a serene smile on her face. Lucy melted my heart. Just adorable.

I settled on the sofa with the iPad, time for some serious shopping. The festivities had inspired me, and working from a list, I ordered all the gifts I needed. Shopping online saved my sanity, I disliked shops at the best of times and at Christmas they were horrendous. With the presents sorted, my next challenge was an outfit for the Masquerade Ball. I wanted something dramatic and different, to fit with the theme of 'Secrets & Guise'. I found the perfect costume, dress, mask, hooded cape, and shoes.

This was going to be fun.

"Have you time for a coffee?" Jessica called from the kitchen.

"Yes please."

I dropped Lucy's overnight bag in the hall and hung up her coat on the rack. I shrugged off my jacket and hung it alongside. I kissed Jessica's proffered cheek as I entered the kitchen. "Good night?"

"Very." Jessica winked

"Don't"—I held up my hand to stop further enlightenment—"when I'm in drought conditions I don't need to hear about what's happening in your bountiful garden."

"Who's doing the garden?" Andrew asked, as he came into the kitchen wearing nothing but grey sweat pants. He sidled up behind his wife, put his arms around her waist, and kissed her neck.

"A-hem." I cleared my throat and pointed to myself. "You have company."

"Aww, are you feeling left out sweetie?" He wrapped his arms around me. "Does Kitty-Cat need some man-hugs?"

I wriggled away and laughed. "Stop it! You smell too good, you're not safe!"

"Has he been at my shower gel again?" Jessica asked

"No, he smells like a man for a change," I said, pushing Andrew away. "Go put some more clothes on. Quickly."

He shimmied out of the kitchen, warbling 'Do you think I'm sexy?' as he went.

"I met with Max yesterday," Jessica said, as Andrew thumped up the stairs. "I offered him the standard contract, which he was delighted with. He saw the poster for the soup kitchen and offered himself up for it, so you'll get to meet him."

"Cool, I feel like I know him already. Have you read it yet?" I asked blowing across my steaming coffee.

Jessica shook her head. "Not yet, I'm going to give it to Kaitlin to edit. She'll be able to clean up the writing while keeping his voice."

"When are you thinking for publication?" I asked. Jessica looked at the calendar on the kitchen wall and jumped along the weeks.

"A.S.A.P, your guys have the info to get a head start. Kaitlin should be free to start next week, taking Christmas into account she'll have the ARC's ready for the end of January, mid-February?" She set warm croissants down between us and I lifted one, grateful my ball gown had laces, not buttons.

"So, late March?" I asked as I scrolled through the diary on my phone.

"Schedule a launch for late April, mid-week, we've been getting good turn outs for them."

"What about the 23rd April? I'd like to be at this one myself and I'll be away after that."

"That's right! Your 40th is the day after. Still refusing a party?" Jessica gave me her puppy dog eyes.

"Definitely. If I have to be 40, I at least want to be on a beach."

Was it too much to hope I might have someone to share it?

CHAPTER 11

December moved in like a scene from Mothercare, a blazing blue sky, pink-edged candyfloss clouds, and a sprinkling of white frost. The first day of advent had its traditions for me, one was the chocolate filled calendar — I would never be too old — the other was decorating my home. These days I used one of our suppliers, 'Occasional Dressing', to transform the flat into my own piece of Christmas heaven, and Samantha arrived at 10am, as scheduled. If Samantha were a season, she would be autumn. Her hair was the colour of ripe horse chestnuts, highlighted with flashes of burnt orange. Oddly, her eyes were exactly the same, chocolate pools flecked with glints of fire. I buzzed her in, the lift doors opened and flooded the landing with the scent of pine, vanilla, and cinnamon.

"Wow, Sam this smells amazing."

She pushed the huge plastic storage box that was the height of her, towards the door. I was grateful it had wheels.

"Doesn't it?" She agreed. "Christmas tree in the same place?" I nodded, opening the doors and standing back to let her, and the cargo, passed.

"Coffee?"

"Oh yes please Cath. I need the caffeine, I was out last night"—she stopped by the window—"although this view would restore you every time."

"Yeah, it is pretty special," I said, as I handed her a cup of Marks & Spencer's Christmas coffee, poured from the pot. "Are you still okay to head up to the cottage and dress it for me? Feel free to stay over, just ring ahead."

"That's great, thanks." Samantha beamed. "I was planning on going up next Sunday, so I might make it Saturday afternoon, if you're not planning on being there?"

"No,"—I handed her the keys—"next Saturday I'm at my first 'Singles Supper Club'." Samantha arched an eyebrow and opened her mouth. I raised my hand. "Don't say a word. Nothing ventured, nothing gained, right?"

"If you say so. You're a braver girl than me, that's for sure." She sipped her coffee. "Are you sure it's legit and not one of those 'throw your keys in the bowl' set-ups?"

"Yes I'm sure!" I laughed. "Although I bet they

were fun in their day too."

"Well, good luck," Samantha said. "You're one of the nicest people I know, it would be so cute to see you loved up."

"Steady on," I laughed. "Mr Right might take some finding. Mr Right-now would be a start."

I diligently followed Samantha's instructions, as she made the design in her head come alive. I loved the traditional colours of Christmas — green, red, and gold — and she unfolded them around us. A huge garland made from pine and ivy draped over the mantelpiece, decorated with sprigs of holly, with its blood red berries, pearls of mistletoe, cinnamon scented golden pinecones, and white Christmas lilies. Stepping back, we surveyed the masterpiece and grinned at each other, before setting about the tree.

It was late into the afternoon before she left. The light outside faded, and the reflection of the twinkling fairy lights danced on the windows. Artificial flames licked up the hearth from the fire and finished my idyllic room off perfectly. It was a scene from a Christmas card, complete with stockings hanging from the mantelpiece, and it was faultless. I nursed a mug of creamy hot chocolate, made with shavings bought from O'Connails at the Christmas market, and watched the mini marshmallows bob gently on the surface, dissolving into a sticky layer.

Frank Sinatra crooned about candy canes, and it being the time of year when the world fell in love. I wished I had someone to share this with, someone to snuggle up to on a winter's night and talk about our hopes and fears. I wasn't sad, it was impossible to feel any sense of melancholy in this fabulous setting. I was wistful — nostalgic almost, not for the past, but for the future I was yet to have.

I thought about Mr Mystery. What was he doing? Where was he, and who was he sharing his dreams with? And there was Max, my heart ached when I thought of him facing Christmas alone this year. Yes, over his lifetime, he had been away from his blood family, but the army had stood in. Even in later years when he had worked Christmas, somewhere in the world the other half of him was under the same moon. This year, he was alone. I had an overwhelming urge to find him, and hug him. I grabbed the iPad.

To : Maxwalker@gmail.com

From : CatherineHarvey@CHP.com

Subject : Re; How Will You Remember Me?

Hi Max

Congratulations!

Delighted to hear about your publishing contract with Ulster Press.

I hear you will be joining us at the soup kitchen on the 20th, and I look forward to meeting you,

Regards

Catherine

Sent from my iPad

The reply came back immediately.

From : Maxwalker@gmail.com

To : CatherineHarvey@CHP.com

Subject : FW Re; How Will You Remember Me?

Hi Catherine

Thank you, it all feels a little surreal.

See you on the 20th,

Max

Sent from my iPhone

I liked his prompt reply, and, for a reason I couldn't explain, I had butterflies. My inner stalker was curious and I typed his name into Google.

Max Walker

Cricketer

Maxwell Henry Norman Walker AM is a former Australian cricketer and VFL/AFL footballer. Formerly an architect, he currently works as a media commentator and motivational speaker and has diverse business interests. Wikipedia

A bespectacled, grey haired gentleman in his mid-sixties did not fit with the image of Max I had in my head. I scrolled down.

Max Walker has 15 books on Goodreads with 86 ratings. Max Walker's most popular book is How to Hypnotise Chooks & Other Great Yarns.

How to Hypnotise Chooks? Seriously? I laughed and shook my head. "Brilliant!"

I searched on. Nothing. No Facebook, no Twitter, no LinkedIn. No obvious internet presence at all. Given his line of work, it was understandable he would protect his identity, but this was frustrating. How was I supposed to stalk him? The 20th was ages away. I groaned; I considered myself to be patient, until I had to wait for anything.

Another working week passed in a blur of activity, finalising the arrangements for the Christmas events schedule. Corporate festivities, private parties, even a celebrity wedding, and the biggest event of the year 'Secrets & Guise', The Masquerade Ball in the Titanic building on New Year's Eve. We organised hundreds of events a year, but this one was special; sold out for weeks, and everything was ready to roll.

"Meg, you're heading up operations. Sam's team are in doing the decorations from the 30th and you're their contact, yes?"

Meg nodded. "I'm skiing over Christmas, but I'm back on the 29th. Chris is deputising and has been briefed."

"Okay, any problems let me know. You have the security team booked with G4S?" I asked, and again Meg nodded, draining her coffee. "And Titanic are providing the bar and waiting staff?"

"Yeah, also have 'Tuscan Strings' booked to play throughout dinner and 'Taylor Storm' providing music for the dance." Meg read out from her notes. "Your woman from UTV is hosting the fundraising raffle, but she won't be staying on, as she has a personal engagement."

"Are we confident everything is covered?" I asked, seeking complete assurance. "This is a big deal for CHP, and for the charity. I am beyond excited, but I want to experience the event as a guest. It's an ideal opportunity to get some unbiased feedback, as we will be incognito. Right, that's us for another week. Enjoy the weekend and I'll see you all Monday."

I returned to my desk and picked up a message on my mobile from Andrew,

'I can't get away tonight, sorry x'

Looked like I was making my own way over. I packed up my things and dashed out of the offices. I checked my watch — 16:25 — plenty of time to get to the dry cleaners to pick up my dress for tomorrow night's Supper Club.

How Will You Remember Me?

CHAPTER 12

The invitation specified 'Black Tie and Mask', which suited Connor. He didn't need to think about what to wear, and could hide without trying. He preferred to work these occasions, but Megan had asked him to go, and, as an old family friend, he felt obliged. And, it wasn't at though he had anything better to do.

He held his tuxedo up to the light. Cleaned eighteen months ago, after its last outing to the Crown Prince of Abu Dhabi's 50th Birthday, it had travelled half way across the world since. Connor pulled it on to check the fit, surveying his reflection. He looked well in a suit, it was all in the shoulders, and his were broad and strong. He zipped the outfit back into a protective bag and carried it into the hall.

Connor had settled in this apartment. There was enough light and space for him to feel free, not trapped as he might somewhere else. The view across the lough was stunning, liberating even. Belfast ran away across to the left, and the sea ebbed in from the right. The Cave Hill rose before him in silhouetted splendour against the evening sky, the Castle aglow with beams of warm light. He picked up his keys, lifted the suit, and checked his watch — 16:55 — he would catch the dry cleaners downstairs.

Joyce raised her eyes from her copy of Woman's Weekly long enough to register I was a regular.

"What about you, Miss Harvey? Life treating you well?"

I had given up insisting she call me Catherine.

"Very well, thanks, and you? All ready for Christmas?"

Joyce gave me the run down on her plans to visit her eldest son and his family in Scotland, as she located my dry cleaning and laid it over the counter.

"Put your wee card in there." She offered me the machine. "Now your PIN, lovey," she said, dramatically turning her face to the wall.

I entered my number and my nail caught on the edge of the button. I yelped as it tore low down.

"Oh that looks sore. Go on through to the bathroom, right to the end on the left, there's a nail kit under the sink." Nursing my hand like my finger was broken, I went down the hallway as directed. The doorbell jingled.

"Good evening Sir, How can I help?" Joyce sang out. I giggled, must be a new customer.

The door chimed Connor's arrival. Harsh, chemical-laced air filled his nose, and he entered the Dry Cleaners. The woman behind the counter greeted him, and he handed over the suit bag.

"Could you have this cleaned for me please, Joyce," he asked, noting her name badge. Connor smiled and Joyce blushed.

"Certainly Sir"—she handed him the order form— "fill this wee form in for me, is next Friday soon enough?"

"Perfect," he assured her, taking his ticket. "Thanks, Joyce, See you next week."

Connor heard heels clicking up the corridor from the back of the store as he pulled open the front door. The darkness enveloped him, cold air nipped around his face and ears. He jogged to the entrance of the apartment block and slipped in to the warm lobby. The security guarded nodded a greeting, and Connor stepped into the waiting lift.

Disaster averted, I re-joined Joyce in the front of the shop and displayed my stumpy nail.

"I'll need a false one on there I think Joyce." I looked up. "Are you okay? You're a little flushed."

"Oh Lassie," she exclaimed, her hand on her chest.

"You missed a rare treat. Beautiful man, would remind you of that Michael Fass-wotsit. If only I was twenty years younger."

She was still sighing as I left, carrying my dress over my arm, laptop bag over my shoulder, and rummaging for my keys, I entered the lobby of the apartment block. The lift doors slid closed.

"Wait up!"

"Too late," John commiserated from the security desk.

"Hi John, no rugby tonight?" He looked furtively over each shoulder before raising his iPhone above the desk.

"Working 'til ten so I'll be watching online." He winked and held his finger up to his lips. "Shhhh!"

I laughed and winked back. "Your secrets safe with me."

The lift was back and I stepped in to a lingering cloud of aftershave. His aftershave. It pulled me back to the church, the smell of him embedded in my memory. I blew out a steadying stream of breath to release the knot that had formed deep in my stomach. Damn, he was going to take some forgetting.

I changed, pulling on an Ulster Rugby top and jeans, hoping Jessica would leave the game on, even if Andrew was delayed. I was a massive fan. There was something exhilarating about the power of the men on the pitch. Fit and fearless, the players charged headlong into the opposition with an unwavering determination to get the ball over the line. The atmosphere at their home ground was electric, the support for the home team incredible; to fully appreciate it, it needed to be experienced.

I checked the time, six pm. I would walk to the hotel on the corner and get a taxi from the rank there. I pushed open the door to exit the apartment block and there was Andrew, phone in hand, coming round to the passenger side of his parked car.

"Hey, your psychic abilities are strong today, I was about to text you." He opened the door. I was confused. I hadn't expected him, but there was something else. Andrew was different. I stepped into his offered embrace.

"I was going to get a taxi, I thought from your text you couldn't get away."

I felt him stiffen, and stepped back to look at his face. His lips curled to a smile, but he was tense.

"Oh right, yes… erm, awkward client. Sorry, I figured if I got here for six it would be cool."

"It is." I got into the passenger side. He shut the door and walked round the front of the car. I watched him. "What's different?" I asked. He paled, visibly.

"What? What do you mean?" He was uncomfortable. "Nothing's different, what would be different?"

"Your hair's shorter, and you've lost weight." He relaxed. "You look… sharper." There was more to it, but I couldn't put my finger on it. I changed the subject to something he could handle. "So, you looking forward to the game?"

Saturday dawned dry and bright, a deceptive day whose breath would strip the skin from your face with its icy lick. I wasn't planning to leave the flat until the evening, so I was happy to believe the lie out of the window and enjoy the brilliant blue sky. I had a box of Christmas cards to sign that would take most of the day, but coffee was percolating, Dean Martin sang of his dreams of a White Christmas, and all was well in my little world.

I thought back to last night. Andrew had took Lucy to bed after we watched the Ulster Men romp to victory against the Leicester Tigers, and I got a chance to speak to Jessica. She had assured me he was fine, he had been working long hours with an end of year dead line looming in the world of accountancy. I wasn't as convinced as she was — something was irritating my intuition — but I had no clues and didn't want to start digging.

I made it to the end of the box with a sense of satisfaction and a bad case of cramp. I unzipped the dry cleaning bag, and hung the dress in the bathroom. I adored this dress. A red pull-on Donna Karan, three-quarter length sleeves with a cross over front. It clung unforgivingly, but looked amazing, and with the help of some good underwear, and having dropped a couple of pounds after the accident, I could get away with it for tonight. I wanted to make the right impression — classy, but fun, self-sufficient, but inviting — and this dress was perfect.

I showered, moisturised everything, and dried my hair, before shimmying into a body shaper, and pulling the beautiful red dress over my head. It was a modest length, sitting below the knee, and I finished with some sheer hold ups and strappy sandals. I pulled my hair into a smooth chignon; my fringe covered my healing scar. I twisted side to side in the full-length mirror and was delighted with the results. I felt comfortable and looked good. Perfect.

Today was a good day. Connor had a new car of his own. Not hired, or provided as part of a job, one of his very own. He pulled out of the showroom, appraising the reflection of the Audi A5 Coupe. Its sleek form coated in pearl effect Daytona Grey, inside was a heady mix of leather and excitement. Ready to harness the power beneath his hands, he caressed the steering wheel with light feather-like touches. Connor grinned; he just wanted to drive. He pushed on the radio, 'Bat Out Of Hell' pumped out and he cranked it up, laughing, as he hadn't laughed in years. He knew exactly where he was going.

Connor pulled onto the M1 and headed west. It was a fine day to drive, cold but clear. His face was a mask of pure enjoyment. The car, the scenery, life as it was in this moment. He reached his destination and pulled up opposite the entrance. There was a car in the drive, the boot open, and he waited in his seat. Watching. Surveying the scene. It was hard to break the habits of a lifetime. A woman came out of the cottage, retrieving armfuls of greenery from the boot, and disappeared inside. Connor got out of the car and walked across the road, stretching. The woman appeared, she was nervous, he could smell it, and he stopped a comfortable distance away. Her body relaxed and she smiled.

Connor raised his hand in greeting as he continued towards her.

"Hi there, how's it going?"

"Grand," she replied. "Can I help you with something?"

"Is this your place?" Connor asked, pointing to the cottage, his hand shading his eyes.

"I wish! It belongs to a client." She thumbed towards the Christmas decorations in the boot. "I'm dressing the place for her."

"Ah, I see. It used to belong to my parents, years back. We spent summer's here when we were kids. Do you know if she rents it out? It would be good to stay again, you know, re-visit the memories?" Grief darkened his eyes, fleetingly.

"Not that I know of, but if you want to leave me your contact details I can pass them on, would that do?"

"That would be great, thanks." Connor passed her his card. Name, number. Simple. "Cheerio."

He raised a hand and turned, aware of her eyes on him as he walked back to his car.

Driving back to Belfast, Connor acknowledged things were starting to fall into place. The apartment, the project, the car, all dropping into position. He slowed the car on the approach to the underground car park, and pulled the entry pass from his wallet. The photo. It was still there, a reminder to live life with no regrets. Connor pulled away under the barrier, he caught a glimpse of a shapely calf and a blur of red stepping out of the apartments onto the pavement as he disappeared into the underbelly of the block.

How Will You Remember Me?

CHAPTER 13

The taxi tooted its arrival.

"That's me John. See you tomorrow," I said. A new Audi A5 crawled passed and down into the residents car park. I whistled appreciatively. "Wow, did you see that? Someone has taste."

"And money! You have a good evening."

We pulled up outside the restaurant dead on 8 o'clock. I paid the driver, checked my makeup, and headed inside, to the function room upstairs.

Paula greeted me warmly, and handed me something sparkling. She excused herself before ringing a small gold bell to get the attention of the guests, milling in the hallway.

"Ladies and Gentleman," Paula's voice boomed, silencing the low hum of chatter. "Thank you for coming this evening. For the benefit of the newbies, I would like to take a moment to run through the procedures.

"There are thirty of us here this evening — a full house I'm glad to say — and inside the function room you will find five dining tables, each set for six diners. There is no table plan, take any seat — although please adhere to rule of three men, three women per table. We will have five courses, and you will change tables after each course, at the ringing of the bell.

"Please try to mix up the tables so you are sitting with new people each time, and this will give us all a chance to mingle. No requests for dates this evening as, refusal often offends, and please, no groping, as a slap in the face will offend more than a refusal." Laughter rippled through the assembled group. "Drop me an email, at your convenience, and I will approach the person of interest on your behalf and we can take it from there.

"The most important part of this evening is you enjoy it and have fun. We have two new ladies and three new gentlemen this evening, so, if you would like to join me at table one first, I can ensure you get off to a good start, and answer any questions. Thank you."

We filed in after her and took our places at the beautifully decorated tables, with Christmas themed centre pieces. Fairy light curtains adorned the walls, and a tree, with all its finery, took pride of place next to an open fireplace. Chunky church candles flickered around the room and the lights were low.

"Paula this room is stunning," I said, genuinely impressed. "Did you do it yourself?"

"Good God, no," Paula whispered. "I have spent all day in the beauty salon; some of us need the help. I use Occasional Dressing. Sam's away this weekend so Jenna did it, and she's done a great job."

We seated ourselves around the table and made our own introductions. There was Antony in medicine, Phil in property, Simon in manufacturing, and Connie in retail, as well as Paula and me. All vague, but enough to start a conversation which was steered to general topics by Paula. Current affairs, Christmas, the continental market, social media, and I saw what she was doing. People were being encouraged to express a personal opinion, so, while you might not know the name of their dog, or if they have been married before, or had children, you did find out if their likes, and dislikes, matched yours. I was impressed. Paula knew what she was doing here, and that was the reason for the success of this operation.

I relaxed, enjoying the amazing food and good conversation. I wasn't sure what I expected, but it was turning into a great night. It was a pleasure to experience a social occasion I hadn't seen in the planning stages for months, that someone else's blood, sweat, and tears had gone into creating. I forgot about the purpose of the evening and immersed myself in conversations, as we moved around the tables. Over coffee, I looked at the potential. Everyone had been great company but in terms of attractiveness, there was one guy who was cute. Simon was around six foot tall, carrying more weight than he was comfortable with, evidenced as he pulled at his jacket and checked the buttons on his shirt. I thought it suited him. He had kind eyes and a full, trimmed beard. His humour shone through, and he had me laughing hard when he was reminiscing about some of the disasters he had encountered in his 'Tales of Christmas Past'.

"Well, what did you think?" Paula asked, as the guests said their goodbyes. "Will you be back?"

"Yes, I had a great night," I answered, and I meant it. "Do you have any spare capacity at the minute, work wise?"

"I have a good bit of time on my hands. Organising the club events keeps me ticking over, but not busy," Paula said. "Until recently, it suited me, I could look after Mum, but she passed a few months ago, and I'm at a bit of a loose end"

"Call me on Monday," I said. "We'll set up a meeting with the events team. They are stretched at present and could use your organisational skills, I'm sure we could put some work your way."

"Thanks Catherine, I'd appreciate that." She hugged me.

"Not at all, credit where it's due," I said, returning the embrace. "This is an impressive set up you're running. We'll chat Monday."

I ordered a taxi, headed down the stairs, and nipped into the ladies. Two girls — early twenties — were fixing their make-up in the mirror, oblivious to me. The dark-haired one wore skinny jeans, vest top, and blazer, the other had bleached blonde hair, piled on top of her head, and was poured into a black and white bodycon dress. The brunette cleared her lipstick from the corners of her mouth, as I entered into a cubicle.

"You know, as well as being a senior partner at our office that he's married?" asked the brunette

"I'd say that's his problem, not mine," the blonde retorted, "I'm single and he's loaded, and I'd bet I'm more fun than his boring wife."

I didn't like Blondie and pulled a face at her through the door.

"Sure, when I'm his mistress I won't need a stupid admin job anyway. He's resisted my advances so far," she conceded, "but he's had a good bit to drink, and his defences are down in the crowd. Tonight might be the night."

I rolled my eyes, pitying her unwitting victim.

I had enjoyed my evening and didn't want to go home. I text Jessica to see what she was up to. The reply came back,

'Watching TV, Lucy's in bed, Andy's out. I have wine. Come on over xx'.

I flushed the chain and stepped out to wash my hands.

"Have you been texting him?" the Brunette continued.

"Yeah, innocent enough so far," Blondie answered, as she slathered red gloss on her inflated lips. "I thought I had him last night but he couldn't get away. He ended up sending a text meant for me to his wife's best friend!"

My stomach flipped. The girls left, giggling, with Blondie warbling a rendition of 'Tonight I'm Yours'. I checked my mobile and read the text I'd received from Andrew the night before.

'I can't get away tonight, sorry x'.

No wonder he had been so confused, the text hadn't been for me. A mix of disbelief and fury coursed through me, what the hell was he playing at?

I went down to the bar and peered through the bar doors. Andrew had a stupid grin on his face, he was well on the way to one too many. Blondie swayed over and lowered herself on to his knee. He gripped her firmly by the hips, and pulled her across to sit beside him. She pouted. She had obviously expected him to be more accommodating. Andrew stopped grinning, as realisation slapped him. He was in deep. Blondie ran her hand over his thigh.

'Play along' I messaged him.

He lifted his mobile from his shirt pocket and frowned at the screen. I pulled the front of my dress down and appraised my cleavage, 'looking good girls'. I took a deep breath, pushed through the bar doors, and strode to where they were seated.

"Excuse me, but it is Andrew Nelson, isn't it?" —I leant forward—"I'm a huge fan." I flashed my best smile, and eyed him in a way you should never look at your best friend's husband. "Can I buy you a drink?"

Andrew got to his feet, grinning again.

"Err, where you going?" Blondie asked Andrew. Grabbing his arm, she glared at me. "You know he's married?"

I laughed. "Honey, when I'm finished with him, he won't remember his own name, never mind hers." With a wink, I hooked my finger behind Andrews belt buckle and walked out, pulling him behind me. She protested as I dragged her meal ticket out of the pub, but she was smart enough to know she stood no chance against a determined woman wearing a £2,000 dress.

I bundled Andrew into my waiting taxi.

"What the fuck are you playing at?" I exploded, helping him with his seatbelt. Andrew paled.

"I swear nothing has happened. I love Jess; you know that. I thought Karen was just being friendly, until just then."

He ran his hands over his head and blew out his relief at a lucky escape. I tried to check my fury; it wasn't all aimed at him. Echoes of Jack and the barmaid taunted me, the familiar ache of betrayal rippled through me.

I rubbed his shoulder. "I know nothing happened, I overheard them plotting your demise. But Andrew, you are a good-looking guy, and your friendliness could be mistaken for flirtation. You need to be careful."

"I will," he grinned, sheepishly. "Thank you for rescuing me; you're my knight in shining armour." He leaned over to kiss my forehead.

"Which makes you the dickhead in distress," I muttered.

"And you look incredible," Andrew continued, oblivious. "How the hell are you still single?"

"Choice, Andy. Men keep reminding me of how stupid they are," I replied, shaking my head. I laughed as the pointed comment wiped the grin from his face.

Andrew was a near perfect husband, and if he could be led astray, even if it took strong coercion, then any man could be. What was I even doing going to a singles night? I didn't want to take the risk again.

CHAPTER 14

After spending Sunday cocooned in the flat, nursing a hangover, Monday dawned with a streak of bravery. I emailed Paula and requested a date with Simon for next Saturday, the 14th. By 10am, my first date was booked. Simon had suggested the Golden Cage, a place in the city with delicious, simple food, accommodating staff, and fabulous range of cocktails. I couldn't have picked better. It was a friendly venue whose quirky décor would provide a conversation topic if all else failed.

The working week passed in the usual blur. The mounting excitement was palpable; the festivities were almost upon us. The staff were looking forward to the annual stint at the soup kitchen, and the inevitable messy night that would follow. Many were returning to their family homes for Christmas, a few were off on holidays — some to sun, others to snow — and some wanted a couple of weeks off work to relax. I fell into the latter category, although I would spend Christmas with The Nelsons in Donegal, and work New Year's Eve. The rest of the time, I intended to recharge the batteries.

Saturday arrived, and I couldn't decide whether I was nervous or excited. I flickered between them. I wasn't sure what to wear, should I go glam, or was smart-casual more appropriate for a first date? It had been too long, and I no longer knew the protocol. I wasn't sure I should be doing this at all, particularly after Andrew's near miss with infidelity. I hadn't said anything to Jessica, and I felt guilty.

I stood in front of my open wardrobe, hair in heated rollers, freshly showered, in a bra and pants that matched the colour of my eyes. I was refusing to acknowledge the significance of this, I mean, it wasn't as if I expected Simon to see them tonight, was it? Not on the first date... I was being practical, I assured myself, better prepared for any situation than kicking myself with regret.

I decided on smart-casual. Skinny jeans, a teal, chiffon vest top, encrusted with sparkling jewels at the neckline, which cast a glittering reflection onto my moisturised décolletage. A well-cut, long-line blazer and flat shoes finished me off. My make-up was light, and I let my hair fall around my shoulders in soft, loose curls. I inspected my image in the mirror. That would do.

At the restaurant, I hovered at the entrance,

scanning the tables for a glimpse of my date. Connie, the proprietor, smiled as she came to greet me.

"Catherine, lovely to see you." She beckoned me to follow her. "Your friend is already here, I've seated you at the back so you don't get interrupted by the traffic at the door."

Connie was a striking woman, over forty, tall and slender with long dark hair and amazing bone structure. Remembering I was often recognised, she had seated us in an alcove at the rear of the restaurant, which offered some privacy. I was grateful for it.

A tight knot formed in my stomach as I followed her, and Simon stood to greet me. He wore jeans, a teal shirt, and blazer; we looked like something from the matching cardigan dating websites. We looked each other up and down, made eye contact, and laughed. The ice shattered, he took me by the shoulders and kissed my cheek in welcome.

"I'm going to take our similar taste as a good omen," he said, as he gestured for me to take a seat in the booth. I removed my jacket and sat down, nerves gone, and took a menu from Connie, thanking her. I ordered a lime cooler, a refreshing creation served in a jam-jar, packed with ice. Simon ordered a lager and we slipped into easy conversation.

The food was good, as was the wine we shared with it, and I learnt more about my date as we chatted amicably. He worked in manufacturing, but his passion was acting. He had appeared in several productions and had signed to one of the agencies we worked with. A fellow rugby enthusiast who never missed an episode of Dr. Who, and was an avid wresting fan. A mental image of him in a leotard holding me in a double-leg-nelson flittered across my mind's eye, and I drowned a giggle in my wine glass. Simon was a storyteller, which had been evident from the Singles Club dinner. He told tales from his acting jobs, not in a show-off way, if anything he was self-deprecating. He recounted his exploits into cringe-worthy territory, and reminisced about complete fuck-ups he had been involved in. And there were many, each as hilarious as the last, and my face ached with laughter.

The night was over far too quickly. We left the Golden Cage arm in arm, as if we had known each other for years. We shared a taxi, and he dropped me off first, with no suggestion of coming in for 'coffee'. We agreed on a second date, and swapped numbers to arrange it. He stepped out of the taxi to give me a hug, and kissed my cheek, watching as I went into the apartment block, and raised a hand in farewell.

As instructed, I called Jessica when I got home. She answered on the second ring.

"Hi Jess, I'm home safe, and I'm alone," I reported.

"Alone?" she sounded disappointed. "No juicy bits?"

"No juice," I laughed as I shrugged off my blazer. "Although he showed great promise. Rugby fan, well-dressed, funny, good conversation."

"But? Cut to the chase. Married? Bankrupt? One Direction fan?"

"Well, there is one thing…"

"I knew it! Cross dresser? Lives with his mother, what?"

"He's a big WWE fan."

"WWE? Like 'The Undertaker', and all that?" she asked. "How old is he, Cat, 15? I'm not sure it's wholly appropriate for a grown man to be into that wrestling."

As I talked to Jessica, one thing had struck me. While Simon and I had a lot in common, and he had a great sense of humour and engaging personality, there was no real attraction. Not that he was unattractive, he was cute, and he ticked the boxes. Tall, dark, and handsome with blue eyes, and he looked like he could throw you around the bedroom, but there wasn't the elusive chemistry. The spark was not there. Would it develop in time? Was it something that grew, or was it always there from the start? I would see him again, and, if nothing else, I would have made a good friend.

I spent Sunday wrapping Christmas presents. Gifts for Elizabeth's family had been delivered direct, now wrapped and under her tree. I missed my sister. She was fifteen years older than I with a different lifestyle was, but we had a natural affinity. There was none of the sibling rivalry, which often tainted family relationships. We didn't have to vie for the attention of our parents, as they weren't there, and the love of our Grandparent's was plentiful. Elizabeth had grown-up children, a boy and girl, and was a Grandmother, a fact that still amused me; Liz was someone's Nana.

The accident had reminded me we never knew what was around the corner, and I didn't want any regrets. I needed to make more of an effort to get across the water this coming year. I had the money; I would make the time. What was it Harold Kushner said? 'No one ever said on their death bed I wish I'd spent more time at the office'. I was turning forty soon, the realisation I had probably lived most of my life was disturbing. I wanted to focus on me — not in a selfish way — but in a self-fulfilling way, with the focus on my life and the people in it.

I wanted to nurture the emotional freedom that had been growing since Jack's passing. A wave of guilt washed over me. Laura was facing Christmas without him, and I had barely given her a second thought. What had given me a new lease of life had left her bereft. Thoughts of Jack's death led me to my mysterious man. I closed my eyes. I could still see, and smell, him with such clarity in my head. I had locked thoughts of him away to preserve my sanity, but he filled my dreams in the dark of the night, warming me from the inside.

I wondered if Max had plans for Christmas. I felt a real connection to the guy, no doubt, because I had an uncensored view of his history, his hopes and fears, his pain. I felt more grief for him and his loss, than I did for the death of my ex-husband. I'm sure I would be a therapist's wet dream if I laid my neuroses on their couch. But, it was what it was. I would not apologise for it, nor feel guilty. I was excited to meet him, and I didn't like to think of him alone over the holidays. Was it appropriate to invite him to spend Christmas with us? I had seen into his soul, but he didn't know me at all, and barely knew Jessica. It could appear a bit stalker-ish. I still had no idea what he looked like and, thanks to Google, when I thought of him I pictured a sixty-odd year old Australian cricketer.

How Will You Remember Me?

CHAPTER 15

Friday blew in with vengeance. High winds and squally rain made me long for the wild coast of Donegal. It was hairy enough seven floors up on the edge of the lough. The windows bowed in their frames, yielding against the gale's force. I drew the curtains before I left, if they did blow in, I could clean up easier.

Festooned in the obligatory Christmas jumper, complete with flashing lights, I headed out to my waiting taxi. No driving for me today, I intended to finish this evening well over the limit.

At the office, everyone was in high spirits. For most, it was the last working day of the year, it was our Christmas night out, and payday — that included a healthy bonus — was early. An array of festive jumpers, happy faces, and shouts of "Merry Christmas!" and "Thank you!" greeted me.

I hung my change of clothes in my dressing room, and checked my emails. Lisa brought fresh coffee, and sat across the desk from me with a list of last minute loose ends and a sack of gifts collected for the soup kitchen.

Soup Kitchen was an unsuitable label. The Hope Centre was much more than that. They provided beds for the homeless, although woefully under capacity for the demand the city had. They offered support services for those struggling with life, a food bank, and the food hall that provided a hot meal every day, for those who couldn't provide for themselves. The centre operated on donations and we regularly ran fundraisers for it, as well as volunteering, en-masse, at this time of year. It was a humbling, yet gratifying experience. We loved it, the guests at the centre became infused with our Christmas spirit, and the regular staff appreciated the extra resources.

I got to work in the kitchen, prepping vegetables, putting potatoes in the oven, taking meat out. The atmosphere captured me, Christmas tunes blasted from the radio as a steady stream of the city's forgotten society filled the dining room. The hall was beautifully decorated — a gift from Occasional Dressing — the centrepiece was a magnificent tree glittering with silver and vibrant blue ornaments, with donated gifts piled underneath. The guests, wet and windswept, peeled off their layers as the unfamiliar heat seeped into their frozen bones.

I waved to Jessica as she bundled through the

centre doors with the Ulster Press staff, their arms laden with more presents, singing a version of 'We Wish You a Merry Christmas' that was barely recognisable over the giggles and chatter. She made her way over and hugged me.

"Where's Max?" I asked, unable to contain my excitement.

"Oh, 'Hello Jess, lovely to see you'…" she mocked, laughing. " I'm not sure; he didn't make the office meet up. Maybe he'll turn up here. Where do you need me?"

The weather was powerful and threatening destruction, debris bounced along the streets. The city was bustling, regardless. The traditional early finish of the Friday before Christmas had colleagues rushing from the office, some to the pub, some home to start the festivities with their families, others braving the stores to finish their Christmas shopping.

Connor checked his watch; he was making good time. He waited at the crossing for the lights to change, analysing his surroundings. Old habits. The two in suits, to his right, were ogling a short-skirted woman ahead of them. In front of him, a woman gripped her child's hand. To his left a young woman, heavily pregnant, held on to the traffic light pole for support. She shifted position, tipping forward slightly for a few seconds, her knuckles paled as her grip tightened.

The lights changed. The green man signalled safety, and those waiting stepped forward to cross.

The young woman cried out and grabbed Connor's arm. Instinctively, he loosened her grip with a turn of his arm, so he held her by the elbow, and placed a hand on her shoulder for support. She buckled as pain ripped through her.

Autopilot.

"It's okay, let's get you sat down," Connor said as he guided her backwards, lowering her gently on to a bench.

Water gushed away and her panic heightened.

"No. Oh God"—she tightened her grip on his arm—"I'm not due, I'm not ready."

"You might not be, but baby is." He tilted her face towards him and looked into her frightened hazel eyes. "We got this, okay? Take some deep breathes and concentrate." Her shoulders dropped as she relaxed into his care. "What's your name, sweetheart?"

"Louise."

"Hello Louise, I'm Connor. How far on are you?"

"I'm only 37 weeks, I'm not due, I'm not—" Louise's voice rose as panic coursed through her.

Connor put his hand on her face, again forcing her to make eye contact with him, to make her concentrate. He pulled out his mobile and dialed an ambulance.

"37 weeks is good, baby is well cooked," He reassured her. "Have you done this before?"

"No, it's our first," she smiled.

He profiled her. English, from the northeast, her accent was familiar. The hospice was in the northeast. He pushed the thought away. Early twenties, possibly an army wife. Her shoulder-length brown hair whipped across her face in the brave wind. The contractions were regular, a couple of minutes apart. The ambulance arrived.

"Please, come with me?" Louise begged, still gripping his arm. "My husband might still be on exercise, I don't want to be on my own."

He nodded. Army wife. Away from her own family and alone. He followed her into the ambulance and held her offered hand. His appointment forgotten, this is where he was most needed.

Her labour progressed, and after the initial panic, she proved to be a natural. Focused, listening to her body, and the instructions of the professionals. He stood at her bedside, still holding her hand. There was no awkwardness, it wasn't his first birth, and he continued to offer calm assurances. Her husband burst into the delivery suite, still in uniform, confusion on his face at the sight of another man supporting his labouring wife. Connor identified himself to the soldier who shook his outstretched hand and thanked him.

No longer needed, Connor stepped out into the corridor, and got a coffee from the machine. It wouldn't take long now, and he waited for the cry of arrival. The soldier emerged — a father now — beaming with pride and Connor offered his congratulations with an embrace.

After feeding what felt like the five thousand, we gathered around the tree to distribute the many gifts.

My head was buried in a sack of presents when there was a tap on my shoulder. I turned to a face so familiar it astounded me. A young man — no more than eighteen years of age — tall and slim, with red-brown hair and green eyes, with freckles splashed across his pale face. He was so like Jack he could have been his son. The tug of recognition pulled at my heart. His eyes narrowed. I was staring at him, my mouth hanging open.

"Sorry," I pulled myself together and offered a smile. "What can I do for you?"

"Umm…" He looked at the floor, shifting his weight from foot to foot, his pale skin flushed. "Am I too late for lunch?"

I took in more of him, his coat was thick, but dirty, and a couple of sizes too big, his boots scuffed, jeans threadbare. He held a woollen hat in his gloved hands. He lifted his gaze.

"Come with me; let's see what we can do."

He smiled and melted my heart. The similarity was uncanny, even in the way he carried himself as we walked to the kitchen. He was a child; he should be with his family, not visiting a place like this for a hot meal.

"Are you here on your own?" I asked. Suspicion clouded his face. "So I know how many dinners to dish out."

He relaxed. "Yes, just me. Can I do anything?" he asked in a soft local burr, removing his layers of clothing as the heat from the ovens warmed him.

"No, you take a seat"—I pointed to a high stool at a makeshift breakfast bar used by the staff— "everything's still warm— sorry, I'm Catherine."

"Dean," he stretched out a hand to me and I took it, his handshake was firm and confident. "Thanks for this, I appreciate it."

"My pleasure," I assured him, and piled the biggest plate I could find with leftovers, he looked like he needed a good feed.

"Wow, this is great."

"Can I get you a drink?" I asked. "Juice, coffee, tea?"

"Juice would be grand," he said. "Tea would be better…"

I laughed. "I'll get you both, it is nearly Christmas."

I pottered about the kitchen while he ate — inhaled would be more accurate — and engaged in chit-chat. His parents died, killed in a car crash, when he was fifteen, and he had spent the last few years in care. With no other relatives, the system had abandoned him when their duty of care ended. I sat with him, as he devoured his dessert, and listened to his dreams of going to Queen's University Belfast, but, at present, survival was his priority. He spent his days looking for work, trying to make his limited income stretch and his nights reading, to escape his reality.

"What do you like to read?" I asked.

"Anything," he replied. "I love how words can take

you away, and form another life in your head, where you can take shelter from your own worries. I've just finished an incredible book, 'Volunteer' by a local guy — Gary something — he said he hopes readers will be inspired to be more, and that's exactly what I want. I want to be more, not have more, be more, does that make sense?"

"It does, very much so." I rummaged in my bag. "I'm back at work on 6th January"—I pushed a business card towards him across the table—"I want you to come and see me. I'm not making any promises, but let's have a chat and see if I can help."

"For real?" he asked, studying the card.

"For real," I laughed, and handed him an envelope. I had intended to leave a personal donation with the centre. "You were a little late for the gift giving so I'll give you what I brought." A little white lie to preserve his dignity. "Use it to see you through Christmas and the New Year, treat yourself a little."

He opened the envelope and his jaw dropped at the cash inside. Twenty-five new £10 notes.

"This is too much," he said, offering the envelope back to me. I closed my hand around his and pushed it back.

"When I was young, much younger than you are now, my parents were killed in a car crash. I was lucky; I had my Grandparents to care for me. But for them, I might have ended up exactly where you are today."

His face flushed again, eyes glassy, he slipped his arms around me and I hugged him, as my shoulder grew damp from his silent tears. Jessica burst into the kitchen.

"There you are— what's up?" she asked, confused. Dean wiped his face and turned to face Jessica. She paled. "Wow, you're the image of—"

"So, you'll come and see me on the 6th? Do you have a mobile?" he nodded. "Cool, give me your number, and I'll be in touch over the holidays."

He gathered his things and placed the envelope deep inside his jeans pocket with a grin, he kissed my cheek, raised a hand to Jessica, and wished us both a "Merry Christmas" as he bounded out of the kitchen, and through the hall doors, into the windy street.

"Jeez, Cat, I'm sure you near shit when you saw him," said Jessica. "That's incredible; he's the image of Jack twenty years ago. He could have been his son! Oh bloody hell, sorry, that was insensitive."

"No, you're right," I agreed. "He could have been his son. Our son. I'm spooked, but there's something about him, Jess. I want to do what I can. I want him to get the life his parents would have wanted for him, the life he wants for himself. Are you still considering taking on a trainee?"

"Yes," said Jessica. "I'm going to advertise after Christmas… but, I don't need to, right?"

"Right," I laughed. "Now, gather the troops and let's get shit-faced!"

How Will You Remember Me?

CHAPTER 16

Late on Sunday, I headed across to Donegal, the car laden with gifts. The Christmas food delivery was due first thing Monday, so I had packed a little food, and enough wine to see me through an apocalyptic event.

As I drove along the familiar route, my thoughts drifted to the Christmas party. A riotous affair that ended up with the usual tales of the one who drank too much and passed out over dinner, the one who drank too much and told a colleague what they thought of them, the one who drank too much and laid the lips on a workmate. Thankfully, I hadn't featured as any of those.

I was pre-occupied by the men in my life. That wasn't exactly right, as none of them were in my life. There was Max. I was disappointed not to have met him. I could rationalise the connection, as his manuscript had allowed me to 'know' him. There was Dean, a chance meeting — serendipitous almost — that provided a childless mother the opportunity to support a motherless son. Again, the connection could be rationalised by the loss of our parents, his remarkable resemblance to Jack, and our love of books.

Then there was him. There was a primal connection, one I couldn't explain. I sensed him, which I knew was ridiculous. But, in the dead of night, I felt his presence nearby. I had paced the flat last night, certain if I stepped outside he would be waiting for me. Out of the window, a lone jogger was visible under the beam of the street lamp for a few seconds, before rhythmically pounding into the blackness, to reappear under the next arc of light. The sight of someone, clearly more nuts than I was, out running at 3:00am, had given me some comfort.

The cottage was stunning; the seasonal scents of pine and cinnamon hit me, as I entered. Wreaths of greenery, berries, and cones decked the hall and doors. The Christmas tree in the lounge glistened, ice white fairy lights twinkled, and the fire burned low in the grate, thanks to the caretaker. On the dining table, a glorious centrepiece of church candles, holly, ivy, and mistletoe. I called Samantha to thank her.

"No, thank you. I stayed the Saturday night and made use of the hot tub, utterly fabulous. It would be worth renting for that alone. Oh yes, a guy called while I was there, asking if you did rentals. I've left his card in the post rack on the kitchen windowsill."

"Okay, thanks. Merry Christmas Sam, I'll catch up with you in the New Year."

I hid the sacks of presents — mostly Lucy's — in my room, and unpacked the supplies before stretching out on the sofa with a plate of nibbles, a glass of wine, and a chick flick. This was going to be a good Christmas.

And it was.

Awake before the sun, the fire crackled, carols played, and Lucy's enchantment at Santa finding her in the wilds of Donegal was infectious. After breakfast, Andrew and I set off for a ramble along the coast, with Lucy in new wellingtons, to give Jessica an hour's peace in the kitchen, at request.

We ambled along, arm in arm.

"Thank you for not telling Jessica about Blondie," Andrew said.

"It wasn't done for your benefit; I just didn't want Jess upset. And, I think you learnt your lesson."

He nodded, stopping to watch the waves crash on the shore below, as I watched Lucy sloshing about in the long grass.

"Have you made progress with your man hunt?" he asked, wincing as I dug an elbow in his ribs.

"Not really, I think I'm too fussy."

"And rightly so Cath, you're too good to be wasted on just any lump of testosterone," Andrew said, "you need to be sure."

"Truth is Andy, I'm lonely. I have my work, and you

129

guys, but there's an emptiness in me." I rested my head on his chest as his arms came around me. "You've always given me hope that nice guys do exist and that there's a chance at a happy ending for me. Don't fuck it up."

We walked back in comfortable silence, as Lucy bounded around us. The day unfolded perfectly. The opulent surroundings, and decadent food and drink, ensured we all cherished the spirit of the season. Ever present was the shadow of Jack, the ghost of Christmas past. His death made me thankful for the chance to spend the holidays with people I loved.

Another Christmas didn't come with a guarantee.

The day after Boxing Day, with Jessica and Co. off to visit Andrew's parents. Alone with my thoughts, I reminisced over the last year and made plans for the new one. Jack's illness and subsequent death had heightened my own sense of mortality. I had questioned my life, and achievements. As ridiculous as it sounded — even in my own head — I felt Dean was a gift from Jack, given to fill the void our child had left. I rang him on Christmas Day, we talked with ease and I was sorry I hadn't invited him to share Christmas with us, but it was too soon. Maybe next year.

"You've done WHAT?" Connor sat upright, startled awake. The brilliant white of the bedroom wall hurt his eyes.

"Broken my ankle," Megan laughed down the line.

"I'm sorry for the rude awakening, but I'm just back in the country."

Connor fell into medic mode. "Are you okay? Did they operate? Have you a cast? Crutches?"

"Yes, yes, yes, and yes," Megan answered. "I'm sore, but I'm fine. Obviously, I can't go to the ball tomorrow, but you can still go."

"No, no." Connor shook his head. "I'll not go without you. I'll have a quiet one."

"Please, go for me if not for yourself. I hate to think of you being alone on New Year's Eve. I let you have Christmas, but not this too. And, you'd be doing me a favour, you could be my eyes and ears, give me a full event report," Megan argued. "I know you wanted to go, to see how it's done if nothing else."

"True," Connor conceded. "Okay, I'll go. For you."

Promising to visit, Connor hung up and sank back into the warm bed. He pulled the navy blue duvet tight around his neck, and buried his face into the soft pillow.

"Five more minutes."

How Will You Remember Me?

CHAPTER 17

"May I take your cape Ma'am?"

The question interrupted my reverie. The lobby of the Titanic building was a mesmeric vision of festivity and light. A huge Christmas tree, resplendent in red and gold, sat proud, centred in the nautical star that adorned the floor space. The heavy scent of cinnamon swirled around the delicate notes of 'White Christmas' as a string quartet played at the foot of the tree.

"Yes, thank you."

I loosened the clasp at my throat and let the cloak slip away over my shoulders. Goosebumps burst forward, delighted by the caress of the black velvet on my bare skin. I shivered at the thrill. My image, reflected in the mirrored glass, offered no essence of familiarity. The boned bodice of my dress glistened with crystals, cinched at the waist, and fell to the floor in soft folds of deep purple silk; a silver masque disguised my face, framed by the coiffured curls of a white wig. I could have stepped out of an 18th century ball. Turning, I put the cloakroom ticket into my purse, twisting the bag's silver link chain through my fingers, and stepped into a wall of muscle.

"Oh, excuse me; I wasn't looking where I was going."

I put my hand on his chest to steady myself. His forearm circled mine, and gently swiped away my palm, and his hand came to rest on my elbow. The movement so fluid I barely registered it.

"Are you okay?"

Deep blue eyes sparkled beneath a metallic silver mask.

"I am." My cheeks flushed. "Thank you, entirely my fault."

"No worries," he said, letting go of my arm.

"Can I take your coat, Sir?" asked the attendant.

He pulled his eyes away from mine, the moment broken. I moved up the stairs to the ballroom as he shrugged off his overcoat.

The event was split over two floors. On the first, guests were seated for dinner; their tables swathed in a sumptuous deep purple cloth, and decked with silverware. 'Note to self: Check the colour scheme of the event before buying outfit'. Service had begun, and I hesitated. Suddenly, I was weary. It would take too much effort to make small talk, and I'd gone passed hunger. I was late, but I was here. I'd thought twice on it, aware it was New Year's Eve and I was going to a ball, alone.

I continued, up the stairs, to the second floor, into the main ballroom. Metallic swathes of silver silk billowed out from the centre of the ceiling, pinned up at the edges of the room by sheets of ice white fairy lights that cascaded down the walls in twinkling rivers. Pillars of purple light beamed up around the room. Tables surrounded the dance floor, which stretched across to the grand staircase — an exact replica from the ill-fated liner. The bar curved around the room, to my right, and I headed to take up residence at the far end.

Setting my handbag on the bar, I maneuvered myself on to a high stool.

"What can I get you?"

"Jameson's and Ginger, please."

A male voice echoed my order. It was the wall of muscle, standing at the other end of the bar.

"May I get this for you?" he said, as he moved towards me. "Call it an apology for getting in your way." His voice was soft, but deep, the accent rich and local.

"Thank you." I smiled, and raised my glass to his.

He clinked it. "Cheers!"

He surveyed the room, and nodded in appreciation as he did so. I surveyed him, also nodding in appreciation.

"This looks good," he remarked.

"Yes it does," I agreed heartily.

He looked fabulous in a tuxedo. Tall and broad-shouldered, he wore it well. In fact, he reminded me of—

"Great décor, and I like the play on words, 'Secrets and Guise', very clever."

"Yes, I thought so. I mean, yes great décor, great words."

"You're not local," he said, a statement rather than a question.

"Not from birth, no," I confirmed. "It's home now, has been for a number of years, I just can't shake the accent."

"And rightly so, does no harm to remember where we come from. Besides," he smirked, "it did Cheryl Cole no harm."

I stiffened. "I'm not a Geordie!"

"I know," he grinned, "but you are easy to wind up. Ready for another?"

"Hell yeah," I laughed. "Might loosen me up a little, eh?"

In to his second drink he said, "I don't know your name."

"It's not a secret," I assured him, "I can tell you if you want to know, but, the anonymity is liberating, don't you think? We could exchange names, make small talk, unload a little baggage even, or we take this unique opportunity to really talk."

He nodded. "I like that idea, I can't remember the last time I had a conversation that was deeper than the sports results."

"It's ironic, in today's age of technology — with so many ways to communicate — we forget to actually talk to people." I took a sip from my glass. "I genuinely believe the rise in depression, and other mental illnesses we hear about, has a lot to do with it. While we are able to connect with people on such a wide scale, we're more isolated because of it."

"Makes perfect sense to me"—his head cocked to the side—"so, what do you want from life," he asked.

"That's a good question. I don't always know what I want, but usually I know what I don't want."

"Okay," he mused, and leaned forward. "What don't you want?"

I dropped my eyes and swirled the amber liquid around the glass, searching for the courage to speak from my heart.

"Be brave," he encouraged. "We have the freedom of tonight, no history, no future, you can be honest."

"The freedom of disguise." I drained the whiskey mix from my glass. "I don't want to be alone. Or maybe, I don't want to be lonely."

It was his turn to look for answers in the bottom of his drink, as he swished the contents over the ice rocks.

"It's okay, I'm not about to make a pass at you."

He reached out covering my hand with his. "No, I didn't think—"

"Relax," I laughed. "I'm teasing. What about you? What do you want?"

"World Peace," he grinned. "Well, that and, I guess, I want to be remembered."

"Remembered?" I asked. "In what way?"

"In any way." He rubbed his hand across the back of his head, his shirt strained. "For something I did, by someone I loved, by someone who loved me."

He drained his glass and signalled to the barman for two more drinks. "I mean, if you died tomorrow, who would remember you? Who would go to your funeral? Life has an unyielding way of carrying on, and a person's existence melts away in the passage of time. Unless there are others who remember them, their life, their achievements. If you aren't fortunate enough to have a partner, or children, how will you be remembered?" The barman placed our drinks down. "Cheers." He paid for them and took a deep gulp from his.

He was right. Jack was no longer in my daily thoughts. Sure, he would be for Laura, but for how long? She was young, and likely to marry again, how long before he was forgotten? And me, I knew hundreds of people, but who would remember me? He made a good point. I drained my drink.

"It's almost Midnight," he said. "Shall we join the crowd on the dance floor, see in the New Year?"

The room had filled, a television screen showed an image of Big Ben, its hands teetering on the edge of

12.

"Yes, come on." I stood, too quickly.

"Ma'am, would you do me the honour of accompanying me?"

I took his offered arm for support. A girlish giggle escaped,

"Why yes, Sir," I said, channeling my inner Doris Day as we walked to the dance floor. "The honour is all mine."

Ten, nine, eight…

We stopped in front of the screen, arms linked. The heat from the crowd was stifling. I stepped closer, and he moved his arm around my shoulder as I slid mine around his waist.

"And, for what it's worth, I'll remember you."

I wobbled on my heels; my alcohol infused legs were rubbery underneath me.

Five, four, three…

"Whoa"—he steadied me, moving his hand down from my shoulder to under my arm—"are you ok?"

"Yes," I blushed. "Sorry, I was fine sat down—"

HAPPY NEW YEAR!

The chorus exploded around us in whoops and cheers, and a rendition of 'Auld Lang Syne' surged from the crowd as they clasped hands.

"Happy New Year," I said, smiling up at him.

"Happy New Year and thank you. This has been

one of the worst years on record. You've ended it on a good note."

"My pleasure, I'm glad I met you."

I pulled him into a hug and kissed his cheek. He felt so solid in my arms. I closed my eyes and inhaled the scent of him. The darkness began to tilt and spin.

"Oh dear"—I stepped away—"I don't feel great."

"Okay, let's get you to the bathroom." He steered me out, towards the toilets.

"Excuse me," he called to a female member of the event security team. "Would you take her inside and make sure she doesn't hurt herself?"

"I'll be fine," I said.

I tottered into the bathroom and emptied the contents of my stomach into the nearest toilet. I felt better. Shaky, but better. I couldn't remember the last time I'd eaten; no wonder the drink had hit me hard. I moved to the sink, cupping cold water into my mouth and swilling away the acidic residue. I chuckled at my reflection, my mask hadn't moved, and if I looked as rough as I felt it was a blessing. I rummaged in my bag for my lipstick and dragged it across my lips. That would have to do.

Gingerly feeling my way along the wall, I steadied myself. He was waiting for me outside.

"Better?" he asked.

"Yes, but it's definitely home time for me."

"Of course, come on, I'll see you to a taxi."

It felt good for a man to take care of me, and one

who appeared to take my trip into Pukesville in his stride. He guided me through the lobby and tightened his grip around me as a photographer's flash exploded in front of us.

"That wasn't my best side," I protested, shielding my eyes.

Taking the cloakroom ticket from my bag, he retrieved my cape, drawing it around my shoulders and fastening the clasp before pulling on his own coat.

"Come on, let's get you home." He ushered me out of the doors and into the crisp beginnings of the New Year.

"It even smells like a new year," I said, inhaling the cold air.

"And what does that smell like?" he asked, laughing as he opened the car door.

"Hope."

He nodded at me, and, for a moment, I thought he was going to kiss me. He put his hand on my head and lowered me into the car.

"Thank you for a memorable evening."

"Thank you for taking care of me."

The door slammed shut, and I gave the taxi driver my address, ignoring his glare of disgust at the short journey.

As he watched her cab pull away, Connor cursed his own valour. It would have been so easy to kiss her. However, he preferred his women sober, or at least able to consent. He'd seen too many nights ruined by alcohol, while working.

He headed down the slipway, towards the apartments. The taxi pulled away from the lights, and passed the college on the corner. The brake lights flashed as they pulled near the apartment block.

'I bet she was sick again.'

Connor smiled.

Hope.

CHAPTER 18

Connor lifted his buzzing mobile from the bedside drawers and frowned at the screen.

Michael.

"Did you pissed the bed?"

"And a Happy New Year to you too," said Michael.

"Back at yer. How's it going? Good night?"

"It was interesting. Are you free later? Food? Pints?" Michael asked.

"Erm, yeah sure, I've no plans. When and where?" Connor swung his legs off the side of the bed and lifted his watch, 10:30am. Wow, he never slept that late. The pile of the blue carpet was soft beneath his feet.

"The Washington opens at one today, will that do?"

"Aye," Connor yawned down the phone as he stretched. "Grand, meet you there?"

"Yeah, see you there."

The tuxedo lay over the blue and white striped chair in the corner of his bedroom. Connor grinned; it had been a good night. From the freedom of anonymity, he had hope.

"Oh, for fuck's sake!"

Connor slapped his forehead. How could he have been so stupid? He didn't get her number. Worse, he didn't even know her name.

Showered and dressed, Connor set off walking down the steps, passed the over-sized wooden benches, and along the edge of the rippling lough, towards the city. The day was clear and bright, a fresh new sky to hang the days of the coming year on. A blank canvas. Hope.

Connor pushed open the door of the Washington Bar. A heady mix of beer, damp, and body odour clung to the stale air. Michael sat by the window, his slim frame silhouetted by the bright afternoon sunlight streaming in through the window. Two glasses, of what looked like whiskey, sat on the table in front of him. He fidgeted with the buttons on his blue and red checked shirt, and stood as Connor approached.

"How's it going?" He clasped Connor's hand, and embraced him.

"Grand, yourself, and Nichola?" Connor asked.

"Yep, all good mate, all good," Michael answered as he sat down. His hand shook as he reached for his drink.

"You're looking a little edgy there Micky," said Connor as he sat facing his friend, clinking the outstretched glass with his own.

"You're not wrong, Connor." Michael slumped back into his seat and ran his hand through his short ginger hair. "I don't even know where to start, or how to tell you or even if I should—"

"Michael"—Connor leant forward, his voice soft and calm—"we've know each other almost thirty years. Start at the beginning."

"Okay." Michael blew out his anxiety and took a gulp of his drink. "We spent last night up in Derry with friends of Nichola. It was the first time I'd met the husband, but it turns out we knew his sister. She was at the party." He paused. "It was Kelly."

"Kelly…?" Connor asked.

"Marie's best mate, Kelly."

Marie.

Cold fingers squeezed at Connor's heart.

Marie.

His childhood sweetheart.

Marie.

The only woman he had ever loved, or trusted.

Marie.

The reason his heart was frozen.

"Right." Connor nodded. He remembered Kelly. Nice girl. He hadn't seen her in what, twenty years? Nineteen for sure.

"Marie was killed in a car accident, some years ago."

"Fuck." Connor lifted his glass, now understanding the need for whiskey.

"Yeah, her and Kenny."

"She was still with Kenny Morrison? That's something I suppose. At least she didn't blow me out of the water for a fling."

Connor wasn't sure how he felt. A long time had passed, and there had been other women, but none had got under his skin as she had. Marie was the one.

"Kelly said they were happy," Michael continued, "as you know, Marie had no family and neither did Kenny, well none you would leave a child with."

"A child?" The cold fingers squeezed again. "Marie and Kenny had a child?"

"Yes, a son, and this is where things get a bit sticky." Connor waited as Michael took another drink; he always had found his courage in a glass.

"Kelly said the boy wasn't Kenny's."

Connor raised his eyebrows and tipped his head. He wasn't surprised, once a cheat.

"Wouldn't put it past her." Connor sipped his whiskey, hoping the warmth would ease the cold feeling in his chest. "But, what's this to do with me?"

"Connor, Kelly said the child might be yours."

Whiskey sprayed across the table.

"What?" yelled Connor, wide eyed. "I've not seen Marie since the day I caught her with Kenny, why would Kelly think he's mine?"

"Kelly was with Marie when she had him. Marie was off her face, and said something about the child being born on his daddy's birthday. Kelly had questioned her about it, but Marie brushed her off. Eventually they drifted apart." Michael rummaged in his pocket and pulled out a crumbled scrap of paper. "He was born on your birthday, 17th November, supposedly a month early."

"I was last with Marie on Valentine's Day that year, I had two days leave and flew home for it," Connor said, holding his face in his hand. "I caught her with Kenny three weeks later."

"So, it is possible?" Michael asked his face pale.

"Jeez, mate I dunno, so I don't. Possible? Yes, I suppose." Connor's mind tingled with 'what ifs'. "Where's the boy now? What happened to him?"

"Not sure, he was coming 15 when they died and ended up in care, but now? No idea." Michael pulled his hands down his face. "See to be honest mate; I thought you'd tell me to catch myself on, that it was shite."

Connor's heart thundered. He closed his eyes,

visions of her long red hair, falling in soft curls around her freckled face, twisted from his locked memory.

Sweet Marie.

Lying, cheating Marie.

A son. How would that even work? A young man who believed his parents were dead, finds out not only was his mother a lying cheat, but he also had a father?

"Michael, we're going to need more whiskey."

"I can't believe you didn't get his number!" Jessica laughed as she put a plate in front of me, piled high with vegetables and roast potatoes. "Help yourself to meat."

"Don't, I have kicked myself all morning." I reached for the roast pork, and poured gravy over my dinner. "Thank you, I am so ready for this, I didn't eat much yesterday."

"You're welcome." She filled up my glass with fresh orange juice. "Besides, keeping dinner for you gave me a great excuse to duck out of going to the Mother-in-Laws with Andy and Lucy."

"Glad I come in useful," I laughed. "You know, going back to last night, it was like I'd known him for years. I was so comfortable. We talked, about stuff that mattered, not the usual crap. I think that, and the fact I ended up royally pissed, made me forget I'd just met him, so, I never thought to get his number."

Jessica sat across from me, elbow on the table, and

chin on hand.

"Well, you know my view Cat, if it's meant to happen—"

"It will!" I chorused.

Jessica grinned. "So what did you talk about?"

"All kinds," I said, washing down a hot roast potato with the cool juice, and going straight back for another. "Communication, depression, life. We drank whiskey, laughed, and saw in the New Year together. His aftershave was gorgeous, so was he. Oh, and then I puked." I grinned at Jessica's shocked face. "These potatoes are good, Jess!"

"I give up with you, girl!" Jessica shook her head.

"Talking to him made me think about Jack, about death." Sobered, I put down my cutlery. "He said he wanted to be remembered, when he dies. It was poetic, you'd have loved him."

"Must be something in the air," Jessica said, clearing my plate. "We updated our wills before Christmas. I tried to talk to him about what we would want when the inevitable happens, but he wouldn't even discuss it. It's silly, we all avoid talking about something because the thought of it is so awful, and yet if we did let people know what we wanted, it would make things easier when the time came."

I frowned. "I guess. Come on then, on the proviso you're not allowed to die until you're at least a hundred, tell me what you want."

"I want lilies — on my coffin — white ones. I want to be buried, with my wedding ring left on, so

149

Lucy has a place to go, to talk to me." Jessica smiled at me and put her hand over mine. I swallowed hard to clear the lump in my throat.

"I want a reading done, and if you're still about I'd expect you to do it — Remember by Christina Rossetti — and I want 'Fields of Gold' playing as I leave."

"Not that you've given it much thought or anything…"

"Sod off." Jessica swiped at me across the table.

"Hey, keep that up Missus, and you might need that reading sooner than you'd like!" I opened my arms, and Jessica stepped into them.

"I'm not so fussy. Burn me, play 'Ain't No Sunshine When She's Gone', and erect a monument in my name, something wholly inappropriate, like a naked man with a huge dick, in the middle of Belfast. So I'll be remembered."

CHAPTER 19

The first working Monday of the New Year, curled its damp, grey fingers around me as I bustled off the street and into the glowing welcome of the office.

"Happy New Year, Miss Harvey," Jenny sang from behind the desk. "I hope it's a prosperous one for us all."

"And to you, Jenny. Did you enjoy the holidays?"

"Yes, grand thanks I—" Jenny, looked over my shoulder, and fixed her best corporate welcome face on. "Good Morning, Can I help you?"

"Err... Jessica Nelson? Please."

I recognised the voice and turned to greet him.

"Dean, welcome!"

He grinned as he brushed down the front of his grey suit jacket, and wriggled the knot on his blue and silver striped tie, transferring his weight from one foot to the other.

"Hey, Catherine. It's great to see a familiar face, I didn't recognise you from behind," he blushed. "This place is wild impressive. Do you work for Mrs Nelson too?"

"No, Ulster Press has the lower floors, we – that is CHP – have the top half. Come on, I'll take you up."

"Tennent Street Station, Detective Deakin speaking."

"Deak? It's Connor Maxwell."

"Max! I'd heard you were back. How's it going?"

"Awk, you know, settling back in. A lot's changed in twenty years mate."

"Is right, the likes of me — Paddy Deakin — a peeler for starters. Listen mate, I was awful sorry to hear about your Brad, he was one of the good guys. We had some laughs back in the day, eh?"

"Aye, remember that Twelfth you two climbed Glasgow Street's bonfire, to rescue the Tricolour, and they near lit the thing with you still in it?" Connor smiled. "Jeez, the fear still grips me. Your Ma would have killed me."

"She would have, she thought you were a good boy, so she did. Well, until you took the Queen's shilling, you weren't so popular after. You can imagine how my career choice sits." Paddy's laughter rattled down the line.

"Deak, I need a favour."

"Sure mate, what can I do for you?"

"I need a trace"—Connor smoothed out the creased piece of paper onto his thigh—"I have a name, a date of birth, I know his parent's names, and I know he went into care about three years ago. What I need to know is where he is now."

"Dead on. Give me what you have and I'll have a look here."

Connor relayed the details, his stomach as crumpled as the note, breath bated. His eyes closed, silently pleading.

"Okay, here he is. Nose is clean so far, he's showing at the Salvation Army's assisted housing project on Victoria Street, Flat 12."

"He's here? In Belfast?" Connor walked to the window and looked out over the lough, towards the city.

"That's what it says here. You alright Max?"

"Yeah," Connor ran his hand over his head, and exhaled in a whistle. "Not what I expected, I suppose."

"Anything else I can do mate?"

"Aye," Connor grinned as the news settled over him. "You can let me buy you a pint, and soon."

"Deal, it will be good to catch up. If you can't catch me here Michael has my mobile, shout when you're free. Good luck."

"Cheers, Deak."

Connor stared out across the cityscape and placed his hand on the cool window. Somewhere, over the majestic outline of Belfast, was — potentially — his son, Dean.

"How the fuck am I going to play this?"

His bewilderment reflected in the glass.

"Relax," Jessica laughed, placing her hand on Dean's shoulder. "We're all house-trained, no-one bites. You're going to love it here."

"I know I will, you've given me an incredible opportunity here and I can't thank you enough." He flashed a smile.

"You're going to be shadowing Kaitlin Winters, one of our editors," said Jessica, as she dialed Kaitlin's extension. "She has been working on the autobiography of a local guy, your homework this week will be to familiarise yourself with his story. You'll be assisting with the remainder of the project."

"That's cool," nodded Dean, his eyes bright with enthusiasm.

"We have that launch at the La Mon tomorrow night Jess," I reminded her. "Would it be worth Dean attending to see what goes on?"

"Sure," said Jessica. "If you're free Dean?"

"Yeah, that's grand, so it is. What time shall I be there for?"

"I'll send a car for you at six," I said, standing as

Jessica waved Kaitlin into the office. "I'll be up there from lunchtime, just ask for me at reception. Right I'll leave you guys to it. Have a great day Dean, call and see me when you finish, let me know how you get on?"

"Will do, and thanks, again," said Dean.

"Pleasure," I returned his infectious grin. "Jess, you'll have the stock ready for tomorrow?"

"Yes, all ready to go. I'll pop upstairs, when I've a minute, to go through the final schedule."

I closed the office door behind me as Dean stood to shake hands with Kaitlin. A wave of warmth washed over me, this young man was special, I knew it — although beyond the familiarity — I wasn't sure why.

Time would tell.

Connor pulled his scarf higher up his face, thankful for the overcoat shielding him from the biting wind that whipped off the River Lagan as he crossed the Queen Elizabeth II Bridge, towards the city. He strode along the embankment, down Donegall Quay, and passed the back of the Royal Mail building. He buried his hands deeper into his pockets, as the cold, damp air searched for an inlet.

Centenary House, the Salvation Army building, occupied the corner of Victoria Street, and was a relatively new build compared to its neighbours. Connor stopped to take in his surroundings. There was no obvious vantage point, and parking was restricted around here. He would have to find somewhere to stand. The doorway of 'The Tea Company' across on Corporation Street would do, he could see both entrances from there.

The blare of a car horn grabbed his attention. A man staggered across the road, waving an attempt at an apology to the driver. Dread gripped Connor. This guy was little more than a child, stained clothes hung from a bony frame, shadows darkened the hollows of his cheeks, and a drug-induced glaze dulled his eyes. He made for the door of the assisted housing, struggling to pull the key fob from his pocket.

'Please, God, no. Don't let that be him.'

"Have you a wee feg, mate."

"No, I don't smoke, err— sorry?"

"Decky." The boy stiffened. "Are you a peeler?"

"No." Connor raised his open palms to Decky, using his body language to diffuse the threat. "I'm looking for Dean, Flat 12?"

"Ah right, he's away out. Started a new job, so he did, he'll not be back 'til the night."

"Cheers, here"—Connor fished in the pocket of his jeans and pulled out a five pound note—"grab yourself a coffee, on me."

"I'd not be one for coffee like, but this will get me ten fegs." Decky's face broke into a grin. "Shall I tell Dean you're after him?"

"No, that's grand. I'll call back, thanks."

Decky walked back across the road in search of a shop, oblivious to the traffic. Connor looked skyward,

'Thank you' he mouthed as relief washed over him. He checked the time, it was early afternoon, and he was heading to Michael's for dinner this evening. It would have to wait until tomorrow.

Dean pulled back the curtains, turbulent clouds rolled across a slate grey sky. On the street below, a woman fought against the wind as it powered between the two large buildings, before diffusing into Custom House Square. At least it was dry.

Lifting his glass from the bedside cabinet, he crossed the small living area to the corner that masqueraded as a kitchen, and put it in the sink. Dean pulled on his fleece, tightened the drawstring around the bottom, and checked himself in the mirror. It looked ridiculous over his suit, but it was better than facing the January squall without it. He flicked off the lights and lifted the ream of paper that Kaitlin had given him the day before, and dropped in down the front of his jacket. He'd been up past 2:00am reading 'How Will You Remember me?' unable to put it down. Max Walker was some guy.

"Holy sh—"

The vicious wind tore the words from Dean's mouth as he stepped outside. He tugged at his zip, willing it to go higher, and buried his face down into the collar. He jogged across the street, weaving through the early morning traffic — already jammed, and turned the corner into Corporation Street. Across the street stood a man, protected from the weather by the doorway, black hat pulled down over his ears, scarf almost meeting it across his face, and cocooned in a long, black overcoat.

'That's what I need right there,' thought Dean, as the cold air lashed his legs. 'A coat like that is top of the list, come pay day.'

Connor was thankful for the shelter of the alcove as pedestrians fought with the elements. He'd been there from before seven, sleep had alluded him as he played out scenarios in his head. How should he contact him? Should he write a letter, explaining what he knew — as Michael had suggested — and leave it to Dean to decide what to do? Should he contact the Salvation Army and ask them to make the introduction? Should he do nothing, leave the lad with his memories, and mind his own damn business? Losing a night's sleep had left him no closer to a decision and so here, he was. Watching. Waiting.

Each time the entrance to the assisted housing opened, he stiffened in anticipation. So far it had brought out a crumpled guy, old before his time, off to search for another bottle of the drink that had ravaged him, and a couple of younger men, each dressed in a street uniform of loose tracksuit bottoms and sweatshirt with the hood pulled around their faces. They'd passed in conversation, oblivious, the English one called the other 'Fra'. They weren't his. By ten past eight he was beginning to question his own sanity as he pulled his hat down to meet his scarf, exposing as little as possible to the harsh air.

The door opened, the resident stopped to brace himself against the unyielding wind. Connor straightened up, this kid looked familiar, but he couldn't place him from this distance. He was dressed for the office, but new to it – the fleece was an afterthought. Connor watched as he filed through the traffic. He frowned, he reminded him of someone. Who was it?

Brad.

He looked like a teenage Brad. Tall, almost gangly, with broad shoulders, he had a strong stride, the same as the one Connor had followed, without hesitation, as a child. Except he wasn't dark-haired like him and Brad. This kid had his mother's colouring.

He felt Dean's eyes on him, the boy was observant – maybe it was in the DNA – and Connor fought to contain himself, battling the reckless want within him to yell 'Dean, I'm your Dad!' across the street. He'd mastered control of his emotions; harnessed them as they had the power to threaten his existence. Now was not the time to let them run riot.

He needed to handle this with sensitivity. The lad was going to be shell-shocked. Connor quelled the rising paternal urge and watched Dean until he was out of sight.

Connor headed right, along Victoria Street, towards the Albert Memorial Clock, which leaned precariously into the wind, a result of its marshy foundations. He turned in to the High Street, walking passed the entrance to the car park, and the In-shops. By the time he reached the taxi rank at Bridge Street he had decided.

He would come back this evening and tell Dean what he knew.

159

How Will You Remember Me?

CHAPTER 20

Connor parked in front of the main entrance to Centenary House, checking his reflection in the glazed exterior as he locked the car. He had chosen his outfit carefully, jeans, blue jumper, and navy jacket; relaxed, non-threatening, easy-going. He needed a good first impression.

Connor checked his watch; it was just before six. He walked around to the side door, his stomach rolled again. He hadn't been this nervous since he was a kid. Number '12' marked the buzzer that would change his life. His finger hovered. He closed his eyes and pressed it. Words danced in his head.

"Hello?"

'Here goes everything.' "Dean?"

"Yes, mate. I'm ready, I'll be right down."

Connor opened his mouth, and closed it again. In none of the scenarios had Dean been expecting him. He couldn't be expecting him.

"Fuck."

Dean bundled out of the building and onto the footpath. His suit jacket over his arm, he fiddled with his tie. He held out his hand to Connor.

"Alright mate? Where did you get parked?"

Connor shook his hand, taking the pause to evaluate the situation.

"Out front," he gestured. "Do you know where we're headed?"

"Oh," Dean stopped and frowned, pulling on his jacket. "La Mon, the La Mon Hotel."

"Okay," said Connor. "We're off to a good start."

"Whoa... nice wheels mate." Dean caressed the paintwork. "Is this the pearl effect?"

"It is," Connor laughed. "You a bit of a petrol head?"

"You could say that – sorry, I don't know your name."

"Connor, fellow enthusiast. Jump in," said Connor, sliding into the car.

Dean put his head back, closed his eyes, and breathed in. "Aww man, smell the leather."

Connor's stomach lurched. In profile, he was the image of Marie. The same straight, sharp nose and sculptured cheek bones, his short auburn hair the exact same shade as hers. For the first time the thought of Marie didn't freeze his chest and he smiled.

"Let's see what she can do eh? Do you drive?" asked Connor, pulling out of the car park and setting off for the bridge.

"Not yet," said Dean, "but I'll start lessons the morra if you fancy letting me behind the wheel. This thing's a dream."

"Aye right, young buck like you would end up wrapped around a tree."

A shadow flickered across Dean's face.

'Shite.' The words were out before Connor had registered their significance.

"So, what has you heading for a swanky hotel the night? Hot date?" asked Connor.

"I wish," Dean grinned. "I'm helping out at an event. Don't get me wrong, the woman I'm meeting is stunning – blonde, curves in all the right places, good heart – but to be fair, she's probably near twice my age. I could put in a word, if yer like."

Connor laughed, and shook his head.

"Dean, I might take you up on that. Lord knows I could use the help." Connor chuckled; he liked this kid.

They continued bantering like old friends, and all too soon, their destination rose from the green fields on the outskirts of the city. The car crunched to a stop at the hotel entrance.

"Do I need to pay you, or sign anything?" Dean asked, "I'm not sure how this works."

"What? Oh, right, no. It's err... taken care off, don't worry about it."

"OK grand, it was good to meet you Connor, see you again?"

"Count on it."

Connor watched Dean walk up the path, at the entrance he turned and raised a hand in farewell. Connor's breath caught in his throat as the familiarity returned. He was sure the lad was a Maxwell. Despite the burning desire to claim Dean as his own, Connor was torn. He seemed to be in a good place, doing well, he had no right to blow his worldwide open.

Reluctantly Connor pulled away, he had to do this right, and do what was best for his son.

Almost half way. I hated January. Okay, hate was too strong a word, but I had a definite dislike for it. The greyness laid heavy on the spirit, and the long, dark nights drained the soul. There had been some brightness this year though. Dean. I smiled; he was proving a hit in his new role, and with me. He had taken to calling in each day, gushing over his learnings, his enthusiasm bubbled over as he talked, waving his arms and bouncing around, re-enacting conversations, and events. I checked my watch, almost 12:30; he'd be here soon.

I logged on to the dating website and checked the inbox.

1 new message

15th January 12:15

Hello,

I'm Tommy, 47, recently separated,

and living in Belfast. I like the

sound of you, fancy a drink?

I peered at his profile picture; a little dated, but he didn't have two heads, so that was a start. Nothing ventured, nothing gained. Why not?

15th January 12:28

Hi Tommy,

Thank you for the message.

Sure, when and where?

15th January 12:29

Alley Cats,

Tomorrow, 6:30pm

15th January 12:30

Suits me.

How will I recognise you?

15th January 12:31

I'll be the rich, handsome one.

"Great, the bloke's a prick."

"Who's a prick?" Dean poked his head around the door.

"Not you, come on in. This guy on a dating website," I said, regretting my impetuousness.

"You're on a dating website?" Dean's mouth hung open. He blushed. "Why?"

I shrugged. "Seemed like a good idea at the time?"

Now, I wasn't so sure.

I glanced at my watch; 18:40, he was late. Punctuality was important, well, to me. Not so important for Tommy, it seemed. Ripples of irritation phased me. I sat on one of the mismatched wooden chairs, and faced the entrance. Alley Cats was a favourite of mine. Behind the oak bar, mirror-backed shelves were laden with an assortment of spirit and liqueur bottles. A line of white teapots and coloured tin mugs waited to be filled with their infamous cocktails. Next to the door, spindly stools surrounded an old piano, used as a table, and through the cream brick alcove, was the newly opened diner.

The door opened, and a voice boomed in. "I don't give a shit if her son's in hospital, how old is he?" Pause. "Seven? I'd been in boarding school for two years by that age. If she's not in tomorrow, sack her."

I shook my head, how did those dinosaurs still get

away with treating people like that? The bilious man puffed himself up in the doorway, before swaggering to the bar. Dinosaur was a fitting description. A halo of steel grey hair erupted from ear to ear, across his otherwise bald head, impressive sprouting eyebrows, and bulbous nose completed the look. He leaned against the wooden bar, and leered at a waitress as she bent over, cleaning a table. Every inch of my flesh crawled. His mobile rang.

"Tommy Fitz here."

Sick burned the back of my throat. This was not the Tommy from the picture, not in this lifetime. This guy was kicking sixty, and struggling to reach past five feet tall. He finished the call, eyes fixed on me, his heavy rasping breath made the hairs on my neck stand on end.

He slithered across the wooden floor, rubber soles squeaking.

"Catherine?" he asked, as he slapped the bottom of a passing waitress, without breaking stride. The waitress protested, but he dismissed her with a flick of his wrist.

"Well," he demanded, "are you Catherine?"

I cleared my throat. "No, I don't think I am, not tonight, no." I gathered my bag and drained my drink.

He leaned in, putting his hand on my shoulder, and in a lecherous growl asked, "Do you want to be?"

"Sweet Jesus, no." I forced him back as I stood, before remembering my manners. "Excuse me, please. There's somewhere I need to be." Away from you.

167

On the wall, to the right of the exit, a quotation, painted in big red letters, mocked me.

'I am the designer of my own catastrophe'

There was never a truer word.

No more online dating for me. I would rather be single for life. To be fair, I would rather be on fire than suffering a first date with Tommy the Triceratops

CHAPTER 21

Lisa knocked as she entered the office. "This month's Ulster Tatler." She passed it across the desk. "There's a great spread from New Year's Eve."

I poured over the pages, glossy images captured the magnificent costumes and sparkling décor of the 'Secrets & Guise' ball. I scanned the photographs, and grinned, this was great exposure for the charity, and for CHP.

"Oh my God, Look!" I pointed. "That's me! That's my costume, and that is the guy I told you about."

Lisa came around the desk and leant over my shoulder.

"Cath, you need a shake. How could you let him

get away?"

"Oh don't," I raised my hand. "Trust me; I have kicked myself a dozen times a day." I studied the picture and shook my head, heavy with self-disgust.

"You look very sultry."

"Lisa," I giggled, "that is not my sultry pose, that's my 'hold-me-tight-so-I-don't-fall-down' pose." I reached for a post-it-note, and marked the page. "I'll send this down to Jess. She'll beat me sensible when she gets a look at him."

We were still laughing as Dean knocked and entered, carrying his lunch.

"Ladies," he bowed his head. "What's the joke?"

"Me, Dean." I closed the magazine. "How's it going?"

He set his lunch on my desk, took off his jacket and loosened his tie. I expected him to pull out a pair of slippers one of these days.

"Going great. Just been in with Jessica there." He flashed a broad grin and lifted his sandwich. "Things are starting to fall into place, and today is pay day."

"Ah, so it is. Jess in today is she?"

Dean nodded. "Meeting," he mumbled, as he demolished his lunch, wiping his mouth with the back of his hand. I tutted and pulled a tissue from the box, shaking my head.

"Sorry," Dean blushed, taking it and wiping his mouth. "My Ma hated that too, so she did. I'd many a clipped ear for it."

The shadow of sorrow in his eyes squeezed at my heart. He rarely mentioned his parents, but when he did the grief he held inside rippled the surface.

"Do you look like her?" I asked, curious. I wanted him to know he could talk, whenever he was ready.

"Aye." He took a battered photograph from his wallet. "That's my folks, there. Marie and Kenny."

I held the cherished picture in my palm, Dean's parents beamed out of it, exuding happiness. Marie Morrison had been a striking woman. Her sharp, elfin features framed with a fiery cascade of red curls, and green eyes twinkled from alabaster skin. Kenny was stocky, with a full beard, his arm curled around his wife's slight shoulders, and she nestled into his broad chest.

"She's beautiful Dean, and so tiny." I handed him back the photograph.

"Yeah," he grinned. "Da used to say, 'And though she be but little, she is fierce'. Probably the only Shakespeare he knew." Dean pressed the picture to his lips, as he had a thousand times before, and put it back in his wallet. A torrent of sadness welled inside me, and my eyes prickled.

"Awk, Dean…"

He looked up; cheeks flushed, and cracked half a smile.

"Quit yer gurning, woman. There's worse off than me. Yes, I miss them, but dwelling on it won't get me anywhere." He stood up, and pushed his wallet into his back pocket. "You're not going to see me on Jeremy Kyle blaming my screw ups on them not

171

being here. If anything, I'm driven because of it. And I have the perfect role model in you to show me I can succeed, even if my folks aren't around."

"Come here you." I stood and pulled him to me. "They did a good job. You're a fine young man. Be proud." I lifted the Ulster Tatler. "Would you take this down to Jessica for me please? Tell her she's not to hurt me." I laughed at his baffled expression. "It's okay, she'll understand."

"I'll take your word for it." He picked up his jacket and cleared his rubbish. "Right, have a good weekend, see you Monday?"

"Yes, you too, take care. You know where I am if you need anything."

He raised his hand as he strode out and sauntered through the main office. Where did he get his height? It certainly wasn't from his parents.

I crunched across the gravelled drive, knocked on Jessica's front door, and walked in, shedding my coat. Lucy danced into the hall with her finger pressed to her lips.

"Shhhhhhh," she whispered. "Mummy's sleeping."

"Oh, okay honey." I hugged her and tip-toed into the lounge. Jessica lay curled up on the sofa. "Where's Daddy?"

"He's at work, but I'm a big girl. I've been drawing."

I smiled as she settled back to her colouring. This was so unlike Jessica, I'd never known her sleep through the day. I crouched next to the sofa.

"Jess, honey." I rubbed her arm. She stirred, stretched, and opened her eyes. Her brow furrowed and she rubbed her face.

Startled, she sat up. "Cath? What are you doing here? What time – Where's Lucy?"

"It's okay, she's here"—I pointed to where Lucy was sitting— "are you alright?"

"I don't know what's wrong with me, I'm so tired. I must be coming down with something." Jessica sank back into the sofa, her face pale against the black leather.

"What time's Andy due in?"

"Late," yawned Jessica. "He's out with the lads."

"Okay, you go to bed. I'll stay over."

"Are you sure? There's food in the fridge, I could do something before-"

"Go!"

Jessica hugged me, and kissed Lucy before wearily trudging up the stairs.

"Just you and me, sweetheart. Have you a colouring book for Auntie Cath?" I stretched out on the grey carpet, propping myself up on my elbow before getting down to the serious business of staying inside the lines.

With Lucy asleep, I poured a glass of red wine, settled on the sofa, and flicked through the movie channels. I wanted action; romantic comedy was not my genre of choice right now. Romantic tragedy would be more suited. With crushing disappointment, I had cancelled my membership to the dating website. It wasn't for me. Maybe romance wasn't for me either. As Jessica would point out, everything happened for a reason; maybe I was destined to be single. Loneliness sloshed in the pit of my stomach. I washed it away with more wine.

It was near midnight when the headlights from the taxi slashed around the room, signalling Andrew was home.

"Hi baby," he called from the hall. "How was your night— hey Cat, you on your own? Where's the wife?" Andrew swayed in front of the marble fireplace, rubbing his hands together as the fire crackled in the cast iron grate. "It's freezing out there!"

"I sent her to bed early. How was your night? Were you behaving yourself?" I grinned. No dinner and enough wine for two had left me warm and woozy.

I pulled my knees up as he sat down next to me. "That wasn't my fault! Your woman left — did I tell you? By all accounts she'd tried it on with others, and here I was thinking I was special."

"You are special." I laughed, and pushed his arm. "You're an amazing husband and father"—I leaned in towards him—"mostly! Women like Blondie see that and want it for themselves.

"I even understand it, who wouldn't want to be loved the way you love Jess? I know I would, and it's easy to get... not jealous, but envious. I'm glad Jess

174

has someone like you, but it emphasises my loneliness."

Andrew lifted his arm up and patted his chest. I curled into him. It was warm, safe. Comfortable.

"I'm sorry you feel like that, sweetie. I've never understood why you weren't snapped up long ago. You're an amazing woman. Intelligent, beautiful, kind and generous, and you know the laws of rugby, what more could any man want?" He tightened his arm around me, and kissed my head. The heat of his breath sent tingles down my spine.

"I'm ready, I guess. I want what you guys have." I looked up, flames from the fire danced in his eyes and shadows licked at his jawline. I traced them with my finger. "I want someone like you."

Time stopped. In the half-light, Andrew's eyes were almost black. I was lost in them. The fire glinted at the danger within, my thumb brushed his soft lips. Alcohol drowned my judgment. My heart beat a warning in my head. 'What the fuck are you doing?' screamed my inner voice. I opened my mouth to speak and Andrew lowered his. I could feel his warm breath on my lips, taste the last whiskey. I closed my eyes. I didn't want this to happen, but I didn't want it to stop.

A floorboard on the landing creaked and the bathroom light clicked on.

I leapt away, and jumped to my feet, hands over my mouth.

"Andrew, I'm so sorry," I whispered, mortified. "That was unforgiveable, I—"

Andrew wobbled as he stood, and shook his head. "No, don't, please. It was just a… a moment, it was… nothing. Nothing happened. Come here, it's Okay."

I relaxed into his hug, something hard pressed into my stomach.

"I hope that's your 'phone."

"Nope…"

I pushed him away, horrified. He raised both hands, laughing.

"I'm joking! Look" —he pulled his mobile from his jeans pocket—"see?"

"Bastard." I shook my head, relieved the tension had dissipated, but wracked with the heat of what could have happened.

The chattering of a magpie, outside the window, stirred me, momentarily disorientated by the apple-white walls of Jessica's guest room. A wave of vomit splashed around the toilet bowl in the bathroom next door. I padded across the thick grey carpet, and opened the bedroom door. A second heave of vomit cascaded into the porcelain.

"You okay in there?" I called. Andrew staggered on to the landing, fastening a towel around his waist. Shame trickled over me.

"Sorry Jess, I didn't know you were here. I feel so rough; I must have been in some state last night."

"You don't remember coming home?" I asked, confused. Was this his way of pretending last night never happened?

"I don't remember leaving the bar." He rubbed his face and grinned. "I'm getting too old for this. I had better go put some clothes on. I can see you're struggling to contain yourself confronted with my near nakedness." He winked and my face burned. His eyes widened and he laughed hard. "Well, look at that! One nil, to me Kitty-cat. Priceless."

I closed the bedroom door and leant against the cold wood. Andrew was many things, but brazen wasn't one of them. He would never have made a quip like that, if he did remember what happened. Would he? Or was he giving them the perfect clean slate? It would take more than that for me to forget. My stomach twisted as the memory washed over me. What was I thinking? I loved Andy, no question, and we had a lot in common – probably more than he and Jess did – but he was off limits. I couldn't even blame the wine; I'd been drunk in his company a thousand times before. Oh God, how was I going to face Jessica?

'Sorry, but while you were upstairs sick, I made a drunken pass at your husband.'

I went into the en-suite and turned on the shower. I glared at my own reflection, furious and disgusted. I stepped into the hot water, and scrubbed at the guilt. Feeling lonely was no excuse. The image of Mr Mystery flittered across my mind's eye. The resurrection of him, even in memory, was powerful, a primal urge pulled at the pit of my stomach.

"Would you get a bloody grip," I scolded myself.

That was the last thing I needed; I was in enough trouble.

CHAPTER 22

The incessant rain lashed from a slate sky, drenching everything in its path. The dry, warm air of Ulster Press' offices was welcome. Connor took off his coat, and wiped his wet face on the sleeve of his blue jumper.

Jessica Nelson stepped out of the lift, her brown hair caught up in a clip, and loose tendrils fell around her delicate features. Her face was pale and drawn, dark circles cupped her tired eyes.

She held out her hand. "Connor, good to see you again. How've you been?"

"I'm good." Connor clasped her hand, afraid to shake it. She looked so fragile. "And you?"

"Awk, you know. Surviving." The smile didn't

reach her eyes. "Come on up, I have something for you."

Seated on a green, quilted leather chair, Connor admired the wood panelled office. The oak shelving, heavy with books, and large desk, had a masculine feel. He was nodding his approval as Jessica returned with coffee.

"This was my father's office," she said, reading his thoughts. "I spent hours here as a child, leafing through the books he, and his father before him, had published. After he died I couldn't bear to change it."

"It's timeless." Connor took his coffee. "Thanks."

Jessica handed him a package wrapped in silver tissue paper. "Open it." She grinned. Her eyes glistened.

Connor tore the paper, revealing a cream coloured hard backed book. Forget-me-nots were scattered over the front, 'How Will You Remember Me? by Connor Maxwell' emblazoned across the cover. This was it. His life to the point he lost Brad, a lasting tribute.

"Wow. This is... beyond incredible. I... Thank you, thank you so much. I can't put into words how much this means to me."

"You don't have to"—Jessica squeezed his hand—"it's written all over your face. I'm pleased you decided to drop the pseudonym."

"I don't need the anonymity now; I'm not going back into security. I've started up a not-for-profit company to continue Brad's work. He was with a similar organisation, helping the homeless, before he got sick."

"That's great," Jessica said. "When it comes to fundraising be sure to give us a shout. Now, this is the schedule for what happens next. Press releases, interviews etcetera in the run up to the launch. Here's your copy." She reached for a set of papers from the corner of her desk.

Connor leaned over and lifted the Ulster Tatler. "How on earth did you recognise me from that?" He peeled away the post-it-note.

"What?" Jessica frowned, and then her eyes widened. "That's you? In this picture, here?"

Connor nodded. "Can you believe I didn't even get her number? Maybe I should organise a 'Search for Cinderella' eh?" He laughed. "There's probably a law against it – extreme stalking."

Jessica's eyes sparkled. "As I always tell my best friend, everything happens for a reason. Everything. You need a little faith in fate'."

"Hmmm, bit wishy-washy for me." He smiled. "Nice idea though."

'OH. MY. GOD.'

Jessica closed her mouth. Connor was the New Year's Eve guy. She wanted to yell 'I know her!', but this was too good, she had to tell Catherine first.

It was unbelievable, but it wasn't the only thing to have shaken her world today. The tiredness had clung all weekend, and this morning she had been sick. She was late, only a few days but late, nevertheless. Her stomach flipped over, from excitement or nausea, she wasn't sure. Fear, more like. She was nearly 40 for Christ's sake; she was too old to have another baby, wasn't she?

It had taken so long to fall with Lucy, and they had been trying. How had this happened? The cottage. New Year, she'd forgotten her pill. Impatience fired her into action. She dialed Catherine's direct line.

"Catherine Harvey."

"Cath, it's me. Have you time for a chat, in say half an hour-ish?"

"Yeah sure. Are you ok? You sound… breathless, or something."

"I'm fabulous. Sick as a dog, but fabulous. I have gossip you will never believe."

"Tell me!"

"Did nobody tell you 'Patience is a virtue'?"

"Nobody that lived."

Jessica grinned. "See you in half an hour, love you."

Pulling on her coat, Jessica rushed out of the door. "Claire, I'm popping to the chemist, and then I'll be in with Catherine."

"That's grand. Oh wait"—Claire lifted her umbrella and held it out—"you'll need this, it's torrential out there."

Out on the street the rain splashed up from the pavement and soaked her tights. Her shoes took in water and her feet squelched with every step, but the smile on her face never slipped. Her thoughts ran away with her, Connor was Catherine's person from the ball! They would be great together. He was handsome, intelligent, strong yet vulnerable – he was ideal. It was fate, serendipity at her best.

Maybe this was fated too. She touched her stomach, what would Andrew say? A rush of pleasure rippled over her. He was an amazing father, and had always wanted more children. What if it was a boy? A son. She didn't even dare to dream, it was too perfect.

Crossing the lights near City Hall, she quickened her pace and ducked into the chemist doorway, shaking the rain from the umbrella. She was in and out in record time, clutching the paper bag. Jessica stepped off the kerb on to the one-way street, tilting the umbrella to look left down Royal Avenue.

"I don't like these roads, Cathal, too many cars."

Mary's voice shook as she gripped the steering wheel, knuckles white. Cathal didn't answer. He never did these days, not since he died, but that hadn't stopped Mary talking to him.

The lights on Great Victoria Street changed to green, and Mary steered the car left, cutting across into the bus lane. A taxi driver leaned heavy on the horn. Mary winced.

"No manners."

She glanced in her rear view mirror to see him gesturing wildly. An old woman looked back at her.

"I know I turn down here somewhere," she

muttered, peering through the rain at street signs she couldn't see, her glasses forgotten on the kitchen table at home.

It had been years since she was last in the city, and Cathal had driven. He made it seem so easy; he had made everything easier.

"There's City Hall, so that must be Royal Avenue on the left!" Elated, she indicated and steered the car around the corner. The horn from the taxi behind cut through her concentration, and she glared into her mirror. "What's his problem—"

She didn't see the one-way sign, or the woman with the umbrella. Mary cried out as the windscreen splintered.

Sirens cut through the hum of the office. My stomach dropped, the sound always unnerved me. I moved to the window and looked across the soaked city skyline. I was unsettled by more than the noise; I had been avoiding Jessica. The guilt weighed heavy, not only for molesting her husband, but also because she was ill, and I should have been looking after her. I checked my watch. She was running late. I took a deep breath, 'Nothing Happened'.

"Penny for them?" I jumped out of my rumination. Dean held up his hands in defence. "Sorry! I didn't mean to scare you."

"No, you're okay, I was miles away." I fixed on a smile and motioned to the sofa. "Fancy a comfy seat?"

Dean set his lunch on the coffee table and perched

on the edge of the sofa, unwrapping his sandwich.

"You sure you're okay? You look... edgy, or something."

"Sirens make me nervous." It wasn't a complete lie. "Have you seen Jess? She was due to call down a while ago."

Dean shook his head, lifting his hand to wipe his mouth before stopping and grabbing a napkin. "Not since first thing, she didn't look well. Maybe she's gone home?"

"No, she would have—" The office door burst open. "Lisa, what is it?" I stood up to steady her as she shook.

She was ashen faced; mascara smudged her eyes. "It's Jessica"—her hand gripped my arm—"she's been knocked over."

"Oh God, is she okay? What... where—"

"There's a taxi on its way for you, I've rang Claire and asked her to get hold of Andrew's PA."

I nodded, my head scrambled.

"Lucy..." Her name caught in my throat. "Dean, can you go up to Claire and ask her to contact Andrew's mum – tell her she needs to collect Lucy from the child-minder if Andrew's not back." I gathered my bag and coat. "Which hospital?"

"The Royal."

Dean ran out of the office, calling over his shoulder, "Don't go anywhere, I'm coming with you."

"It's okay, I'll be fine."

'Please God, let her be alright.'

Adrenaline coursed through me, fighting the surge of fear. My heart pounded in my head.

'I swear I'll never do another stupid fucking thing as long as I live but please, PLEASE make her be okay.'

My hands shook as I tried to log out of my laptop. "Fuck it!" I yelled, slamming down the lid. "Tell Dean to meet me out front."

I ran out of the office, and clattered down the stairs. My mobile rang, digging in my bag I sat down.

"Andrew?" My insides shook with anticipation.

"Where are you?"

"At the office, a taxi's on its way. I'll be with you as soon as I can. Have you heard anything?"

"Nothing." His voice quivered. "She'll be fine, she's a tough cookie. She'll be okay. She has to be."

I closed my eyes. 'Please God, let her be okay.'

"Let me know if you have news."

There was a patron saint of desperate situations – what was his name? – I would pray to him and all the angels if it would help. Jenny was on her feet behind the desk, her hand on the shoulder of a young girl who was sobbing in to a cup of steaming tea.

"Jenny?"

"Maria seen the accident Cath," she whispered, dropping formalities. "She's very shaken."

I walked around the reception desk and dropped

to my knees.

"Maria, did you speak to Jess? Was she ok?"

Maria raised her head. Her black hair was stuck to her head in dripping waves, her dark eyes pooled with tears. She shook her head. Her teeth chattered and mascara streaked her pale face. She wiped away a line of tears. Dark red smudges stained the backs of her fingers, settled in the creases of her skin. My stomach lurched. Jessica was bleeding. Bruised, broken maybe. But bleeding?

No. No, no, no.'

"Catherine?" I startled. Dean took my elbow. "Taxi's here."

The Accident and Emergency department was quiet. The iodine-heavy stench turned my nervous stomach. An old man held a tea towel to his cut head; a young mother rocked a sleeping child. The receptionist looked up.

"Jessica Nelson? She was brought in by ambulance?"

"She's in cubicles. If you'd like to go through those doors, you can wait there. Her husband has just arrived."

"Cat," Andrew rushed to me. He eyed Dean.

"Dean Morrison, I work for your wife, Mr Nelson." They shook hands. "How is she?"

"I don't know." He pulled his hands down his face; his stubble bristled in the silent waiting room.

"What was she doing out of the office?"

"She needed to go to the chemist, I—"

A blonde haired man, not much older than Dean, stepped through the swing doors. He pulled a plastic apron off his blue scrubs and pushed it into a swing bin. He looked drained, and pursed his lips to a tight line in an effort to smile.

"Mr Nelson? I'm Doctor McCartney—"

"How is she Doctor? Is Jess okay?" Andrew stepped towards him, eager for his world to be back on an even keel.

"If you'd like to step in here we can talk privately—"

"There's no need." Andrew waved his direction away, his impatience surfaced.

Pins and needles prickled my finger ends, and blood pounded in my ears. Doctor McCartney removed his gold-rimmed glasses and dropped his head, fear rose in my chest. My pulse raced. My heart pushed into my throat as he steeled himself.

"Mr Nelson, your wife was struck by a car, although her injuries from the impact with the vehicle were minimal."

'Oh thank you, thank you, thank you.'

I had forgotten to breathe, and released it in a steady stream, as relief washed over me.

"She received blunt trauma to the back of her head when she fell, probably from the kerb."

'Wait. What?'

"I'm very sorry, Mr Nelson, Jessica died at the scene. There was nothing we could do."

How Will You Remember Me?

CHAPTER 23

I squinted. The watery sunlight of late January bounced around the yellow walls.

Jessica was dead.

The weight of grief filled my chest, pinning me to the bed. I gasped for air, fighting the suffocating heaviness.

Every morning. A split second of normality before it hit. Again.

The world had no right to be colourful. It was too bright. I turned away from the window, shielding my eyes from the glare. My black dress hung in the corner of the room. Jessica hated me in black.

'How the hell am I going to get through today

Jess?'

There was a soft rap on the bedroom door.

"You decent?" Dean called.

"Yeah, come on ahead." I sighed, pushing myself up. He handed me a coffee and sat on the edge of the bed. "Thanks." Dean hadn't left my side since the hospital on Monday, never asking anything of me, just being there. "Are you going to be okay today?"

He nodded. "It's the first funeral I've been to since—"

"I know. If it's too much, I do understand."

"No," he said, fiercely. "I want to be there, for you. I can never repay Jessica for the opportunity she gave me, doing this goes some way towards it."

"I appreciate it"—I squeezed his arm—"suppose we better get ready."

The funeral suit. Connor unzipped the bag and shook it free.

"Three times in three months."

Three months. Three whole months since he had last seen Brad. As he dressed, memories of the previous funerals, woven into the fibres, hung heavy on him. The shock at Jessica's death still reverberated. It was incomprehensible. One minute he was chatting to her, making plans, half an hour later she was dead.

The sky was unfittingly blue, as he set off towards the city, glad of the walk to clear his head. Memories of Brad played out, flashes of grief cut deep. His emotions were flammable; he needed to distance himself from them if he had a hope of getting through the service. He would pay his respects and get out.

St. Anne's Cathedral rose in Romanesque grandeur from the city centre, its titanium-clad 'Spire of Hope' glinting in the morning light. Regardless of denomination, it was a magnificent building, it had seen over a hundred years of worship and two World Wars, narrowly surviving the Blitz of Belfast in 1941.

Connor was early. He wandered around, taking in the stained glass windows, the intricate mosaics, and the patterned marbled floor that gently rippled up the aisle. He stopped by a military memorial. A Morris Harding sculpture of a soldier, mounted on an oak lectern, guarded a list of the fifty-thousand Irish soldiers who had given their lives in the Great War. Connor straightened and bowed his head.

Whispers of arriving guests broke Connor's silent reverie, and he moved to a seat to watch the service, unnoticed. Always in the background, he preferred it that way. People filed in, a few Connor recognised from the office. It was near time.

"She's here."

The congregation rose in a wave, the soft tones of Eva Cassidy descended over the hushed crowd.

"You'll remember me when the west wind blows, among the fields of barley."

The pallbearers glided up the aisle, her mahogany coffin, dripping in crisp white lilies, rested on their broad shoulders. Behind the coffin, the family huddled together, leaning into each other for support. Connor had walked alone behind Brad. He shook his head. Now was not the time. The coffin was set on the altar and the music drew to a close.

Andrew's trouser hem caught in the heel of his shoe. I could hear Jessica's voice 'What's he like? 42 years old and still can't dress himself'. I tugged it free. He took hold of my hand, his tremors vibrated through me.

The Dean of Belfast began. I had spoken at thousands of events, but this… I needed to step outside of my own head to get this done. I focused on breathing. The ache in my chest hampered the involuntary inflation of my lungs.

'Focus'

"… Catherine, would you like to step up?"

I nodded, and Andrew squeezed my hand. Stepping up to the pulpit, I smoothed the poem out in front of me. I cleared my throat and fixed my eyes above the heads of the congregation.

"Remember me when I am gone away,

Gone far away into the silent land;

When you can no more hold me by the hand,"

A stifled sob broke the silence. I closed my eyes, fighting my own tears.

'Go on, honey, you can do this.'

'No, this is too hard. You shouldn't have asked me.'

A flash of anger spurred me on.

It couldn't be.'

Connor stared at the woman composing herself in the pulpit. It was. He was sure of it. What the hell was she doing here? Who was she? He'd zoned out during the introduction. She began the reading, her voice clear, calm, and very English. Why had she been at Jack's funeral?

'No, it couldn't be. Could it?'

Connor fished in his inside pocket for his wallet. Pulling out the photograph, he looked at the shy teenager, and then at the confident woman, poised when most around were crumbling. Hair colour was different. The heart shaped face was the same. Eyes, yes. Nose, yes.

'Fuck.'

"… Better by far you should forget and smile,

Than that you should remember and be sad."

I sank back into my seat. An easel displayed a framed collage of pictures. Jessica's face beamed out of each of them. With Andrew on their wedding day. Behind her desk at work. Holding Lucy, only a few minutes old. By the Christmas tree at the cottage, opening her presents. In her graduation gown.

I had taken all of them. Each of those smiles was for me. My heartbeat echoed in the emptiness within me, among hundreds of people, yet so lonely. Dean squeezed my arm. I couldn't handle sympathy. I was on the verge of breaking.

Invisible speakers delivered Andrew's chosen song, the piano picked out the melody. He stiffened, and gripped my hand.

"Did I disappoint you or let you down?

Should I be feeling guilty or let the judges frown?"

Guilt.

Was this my punishment? Taken away forever because I couldn't face her?

"You touched my heart you touched my soul.

You changed my life and all my goals."

She had changed my life, given it back to me, provided a platform for me to reach from and achieve my goals.

"I know you well,

I know your smell.

Goodbye my lover.

Goodbye my friend.

You have been the one.

You have been the one for me."

I didn't get to say goodbye. I didn't tell her I loved her. Hot tears surged over my eyelashes.

"I've seen you cry, I've seen you smile.

I've watched you sleeping for a while.

I'd be the father of your child."

Andrew crumpled into me. I pulled his head into my shoulder and felt the heat of his tears run over my hand as his body shook. This is what happened when you let yourself love. It made you weak, vulnerable. Strength had deserted him.

"And I love you, I swear that's true.

I cannot live without you."

The pallbearers lifted Jessica for her final journey. I raised Andrew up, supporting his shuddering frame. I could do this. It would break Jessica's heart to see him like this. Dean walked behind me, Andrew's mother on his arm.

"Are you okay?" I mouthed over my shoulder. He nodded, tight lipped. His eyes were red-rimmed, cheeks damp.

I pulled Andrew to the side in the vestibule, as the congregation filed outside, and held him. I tilted his chin to look me in the eye.

"Take a moment here. Jessica's staff will want to speak to you, are you up to it?"

He nodded. "Yes, I can do it." He straightened himself up, blowing out a controlled breath. "What about you?" He brushed my cheek with his thumb, interrupting the steady stream of silent tears. "I've never seen you cry before Cath."

His strong arms wrapped around me. It felt good. Shame burned deep inside.

"Catherine?"

I freed myself, wiping tears from my nose with the back of my hand. Dean pulled out a tissue. I smiled.

"Thank you."

"I'm going to head on with the ones from work here, unless you need anything?"

"No, thank you. Will you go home after?"

"Yeah, I'll ring you tomorrow?"

"Okay, and thanks again."

"He seems like a good kid," Andrew said, wiping his face as he watched Dean leave the church.

"Yeah, he is. Come on. Let's get this done."

Dean? What the fuck was Dean doing here?

Jack's wife and Dean at the funeral of his publisher? How surreal was this day going to get?

He filed out of the church. The fresh air welcome as he waited for Dean.

"Alright Connor? How's it going?" Dean was pale-faced; his bloodshot eyes evidenced his sadness.

"I'm good," Connor said. They shook hands. "You?"

"Been better, to be fair. Been worse. You coming to the wake?"

"Oh, no. I don't know the family so—"

"No, employees are going round to the Washington. As far as I know it's for you guys too."

"Us guys?" Connor asked, confused.

"Yeah, Catherine's lot."

"Catherine?"

"Catherine. Catherine Harvey, the blonde you were eyeballing in church, you know, who you drive for?"

Pieces rained down on Connor. Jack, his funeral. Her, Catherine. Catherine Harvey. The test reader. Fuck.

"So Jessica was her…?"

"Best friend," Dean filled in, "and my boss. I thought you knew Cath?"

"Yeah, no. Well, kind of." Connor grasped at the threads as they weaved around him. Jack, Dean, Jessica. They all came from Catherine. "Let's get that drink."

Connor clinked Dean's glass and raised a toast to Jessica. The whiskey warmed his gut.

"Thanks Connor. Tough day."

Dean spluttered, and pulled a face. He loosened his black tie, pulled it over his head, and stuffed it in his pocket.

"Yeah." Connor swirled his liquor.

"I lost my parents, a few years ago. This was the first funeral since theirs." Dean stared out of the window, looking into the past. "It's Jessica's daughter I feel for. Still, at least she has a father."

Connor bit his lip, holding his confession in. Dean frowned.

"How was it you picked me up for that event?" Connor met his questioning stare. Frightened of the answer. "I mean if you don't work for Catherine, why were you there?"

Connor drained the rest of his whiskey. "Dean, there's something I have to tell you."

CHAPTER 24

The door opened, and Jessica breezed in. Her eyes shone, hair falling in glossy waves around her face, illuminated by a wide smile.

"Jess…?" My mouth gaped open, head reeling to comprehend how this was even happening.

"It's okay, honey," she said, sitting down next to me on the sofa. "I'm alright now, don't worry."

"I don't understand." Something was wrong.

"Everything happens for a reason, Cat." She pushed a stray hair behind my ear. "Everything."

I reached for her and opened my eyes. I was alone, overwhelmed by the familiar cavernous ache. A potent mix of hate and anger swirled inside me. I was angry with Jessica. She had managed to cross the damn road perfectly well for thirty-nine years, why was that day any different? I hated January, and myself.

It had been seven days since the funeral, eleven since she'd died. Fourteen since I had last seen her. And life continued. I hated that more than anything. The sun had risen, and set. The earth had turned and rain had fallen, regardless of her death, as if she was insignificant.

I was in lockdown. Physically, and mentally. Emotional self-preservation had kicked in and my barriers were down, the hurt locked away. I hadn't left the flat since the funeral, shunning the offer of company. Andrew and Lucy were cosseted in the bosom of his family, and I was alone. It was for the best. I couldn't deal with the platitudes, the clichés. I knew time would heal, but it didn't ease the gut-wrenching, breath-taking pain that tore you apart in the meanwhile. But lockdown did, to a degree.

My mobile vibrated. Dean. Again. I didn't have the mental capacity to deal with conversation. I threw the fleece blanket aside and sat up, stretching. I stood and peered at myself in the mirror. Dark smudges underlined my puffy eyes, and my skin was lined and flaky. My hair was greasy, and I needed a shower.

The hot water burned my skin, washing away the stickiness of a week's neglect. The guilt remained. I couldn't carry on festering in this toxic mixture of grief, loneliness, and self-pity; I needed to take care of myself. There was no one else. Tears pricked at my eyes. I opened the cabinet, moving lotions around, looking for my moisturiser.

"Damn it!"

I pulled on jeans and a hoody, and scraped my wet hair back into a ponytail. I had to go out at some point. Now was as bad a time as any.

Stepping out of the lift, I pushed in my earphones, and avoided eye contact. I got into the back seat of the waiting taxi and gave the driver the destination. Music filled my head, but I wasn't listening, just avoiding the need for small talk. I mumbled my thanks as I paid the fare, and cut through Castle Court. Wind tore along Royal Avenue, biting through my sweatshirt and tugging at my hood. I pushed my hands deep into the pockets and walked on, head down. In the chemist, I made straight for the counter and picked up the moisturiser, ignoring the advances of the sales assistant. I watched two women in front of me in the queue, their heads together, one whispering to the other before they threw their heads back in laughter. A woman walked by, holding her daughter's hand. A man draped his arm around his partner, hugging her to him. Each scene tugged at me, emphasising the absence.

I focused on the floor as I shuffled closer to the till. I pushed the cream across the counter and paid with my card. Grabbing my bag, I pushed through the doors and out into the street. I leaned against the wall, and closed my eyes, ignoring the life carrying on around me, without her.

I wanted to scream, to release the grief that twisted in me. A tornado of pain threatened to render me unstable. I put my hands over my ears, music filtered in.

"A hundred days have made me older

Since the last time that I saw your pretty face"

Jessica's face flashed in my mind, flushed with laughter 'I'm alright now, don't worry' her voice rang in my ears. Her face pale and still, lifeless in the coffin 'Everything happens for a reason. Everything'.

"I'm here without you baby

But you're still on my lonely mind."

Jessica had been there all my adult life. My best friend, my confidante, my support, my lifeline. What would I do without her?

"I think about you baby and I dream about you all the time.

I'm here without you baby

But you're still with me in my dreams

And tonight girl, it's only you and me."

Never again would it be her and me. Never again would I see her, hear her voice, smell her scent. And there was Lucy.

I pushed myself away from the wall, and stumbled to the crossing. Tears blurred my vision. I stabbed at the button at the lights, head down to avoid the shoppers who ambled around me, carefree and ignorant to my pain.

White lilies, tethered to the base of the lights, looked out of place on the traffic-stained street. I frowned, why would—

"Oh God, no."

I looked behind at the chemist. THE chemist. To the crossing. THE crossing. Here. I felt the blood drain from my face. Jessica had stood here. Her last step, taken from here. The world rushed passed me. I grasped at the pole to break my fall as the blackness closed in.

Connor drained his coffee, clearing the aftermath of lunch with Dean onto the tray, and tipped it into the bin. He stepped outside Burger King, on to Royal Avenue, and watched as Dean disappeared behind City Hall, heading back to work.

The news that Connor may be his father had been a shock to Dean, but not unwelcome. He had taken it better than Connor had even dared to hope. Dean had recalled comments from his mum that hadn't made sense at the time; he was 'tall, like his Da' when Kenny was short. The sooner they had the DNA test result, the better.

Connor looked up at the sky, swirling grey above, weighing up whether he dared risk the walk or should grab a taxi. His attention was drawn to the woman, as she launched from the wall outside the chemist. She stumbled forward, unsteady on her feet. Connor moved towards her. He checked for oncoming traffic, and crossed the road. As she fell, he caught her before she hit the ground.

"Okay I've got you." Connor laid her on to the damp ground, plying her into the recovery position.

"Can you hear me?"

She nodded. Her eyes fluttered. Connor moved the hood that half covered her face.

"Catherine?"

She opened her eyes and frowned, squeezed her eyes closed and re-opened them.

"You!"

I was dreaming, wasn't I? Must be. This couldn't be. Him. Here. I was asleep. Had to be. Or dead. Shit! Was I dead? I dug my fingernails into my palm. No, definitely not dead.

"Yes, me." His eyes crinkled at the corners. "Can you stand?"

I nodded. My head reeled with questions, but none I could put into words. I took his out-stretched hand, and allowed him to pull me to my feet.

"I don't understand," I muttered, more to myself than him. "Why are you here? Why were you there?"

"I'll answer all the questions you have in good time, but first let's get you home. You're pale, and you're shaking."

He took off his coat and wrapped it around me. The scent of him wafted over me and I breathed him in.

"When did you last eat?"

"Erm… what day is today?"

"Come on." He guided me across the road and

206

around the corner to the taxi rank. "Where are we going?"

"Titanic apartments, Queen's Road."

"You live there?" he asked, his eyes wide.

"Yes, why are you looking at me like that," I asked, "is something wrong?"

"No, no." His voice deep and calm. "Everything's fine. Things need a bit of explaining. That's all."

We continued in comfortable silence. I glanced sideways at him. He was everything I remembered. And more. The air crackled between us.

"I don't know your name," I said. A relative stranger was taking me home. Without even buying me dinner. I sniggered to myself; Jessica would like that one.

Jess.

Tears came, again. He took my hand and squeezed it.

"I know nothing about you."

"You know more than you think."

He paid the driver and slid back the taxi door, jumped out and helped me down.

We entered the building, and John smiled from behind his desk, nodding a welcome.

"Did you leave the car indoors today?" John asked.

"Aye, didn't fancy risking it. Never know what's in the rain these days!"

"How do you—" I began, confused. "Never mind, all in good time, right?"

"Right. And my name's Connor, Connor Maxwell."

We stepped into the lift and rode to the top floor. I let us into the flat and he followed me into the living room.

"Okay Catherine, you are going to lie down, and I'm going to make you a cup of tea."

"Make it coffee, black?"

"Okay, what about food?"

"I haven't been bothering, with shopping and such. I've had a… difficult couple of weeks."

"Yeah, she's a hell of a loss, for her family, and for you," Connor called over his shoulder, as he walked into the kitchen.

That was true. Wait, he knew about Jessica? The list of questions was getting longer. He carried the coffee in, and set them on the table, sitting next to me on the sofa. I pulled the fleece up to my chin and eyed him. I didn't know where to begin; exhausted I pushed my fringe back and rested my head on my hand.

He tipped his head to the side, and traced the scar along my hairline.

"Recent?" he asked.

"Yeah"—I smoothed the hair back over it— "although, it feels like a lifetime ago." I picked up my coffee. "I was ran off the road, on the way back from

Donegal. It happened over there." I nodded out of the window, across the lough.

Connor stared at me, his mouth hung open.

"Wow, this gets stranger."

"What do you mean?" I asked. "Now would be a good time to answer some of those questions."

"Yeah. Strap yourself in; this is going to get a bit strange. Fated, almost."

'Everything happens for a reason Cat. Everything.'

"Shoot, let me hear it." I sipped my coffee.

"So, as I said, my name is Connor Maxwell, but you will know me better as Max Walker."

I sprayed my coffee over him.

"You're shitting me!" I exclaimed. "You're Max? Jessica's Max?"

"The very same," he laughed, wiping the caffeinated residue off his face. "Jack — I'm guessing your ex-husband?" —I nodded—"was in the hospice with my brother, Brad, which is why I ended up being at his funeral."

"That's an incredible co-incidence, don't you think? You were there, and now you're here, picking me up off the street?" I blushed. "So to speak."

"It's only the tip of the iceberg." He grinned. "An appropriate reference coming from the heart of the Titanic Quarter."

Warmth rubbed at the edges of the hollowness.

"Don't give up the day job," I teased.

"Too late, already have, but that's another story." Connor tucked the fleece in around my knees as he continued. "When I moved back to Belfast, a friend put me in touch with Jessica, and then you got involved. The rest, as far as the book goes, you know. What next"—he rubbed his forehead—"you drive a Black BMW X5?"

I nodded.

Connor pointed out of the window. "That was me, at the crash."

My jaw dropped. Nothing came out.

"I know!" he said. "Maybe Jessica was right."

"What do you mean?"

My chest tightened at the sound of her name on his lips.

"I spoke to her, that day." He covered my hand with his. "There was this magazine and she'd marked a picture of me with a post it note — I'd met a woman at an event and didn't get her number — Jessica said I needed to have a little faith in fate, and that everything happened for a reason. Maybe she was right."

I rummaged in the pile of magazines on the coffee table, pulling out another copy of Ulster Tatler. I flicked through the pages.

"This picture?" I asked, turning it to show him.

"Yes, that's the one!" He peered at the photograph, then at me, and back to the magazine. "Noooooo!"

I nodded. I remembered Jessica's call, the excitement in her voice. I beamed; she would have loved that. Serendipity in full flight.

"Jessica knew?" Connor said, his eyes dancing. "She knew that was you?" He walked over to the window, rubbing his hands over his head and down his face. Turning, he stopped. "This picture" – he pointed to the watercolour of Lucy's Cottage hanging on the wall – "do you know where that is?"

"Yes, it's in Carrick, Donegal. I bought it five, maybe six, years ago."

"Six," Connor said. "My parents owned it until then. I spent every summer of my childhood there."

Goosebumps erupted on my skin. I walked over and stood next to him. The heat of his body radiated through my sweatshirt.

"I dreamt of you, while I was there." My cheeks burned. Did I say that aloud? My inner goddess was a gobshite.

"I called once, and left my card," Connor said, glossing over my embarrassment.

"I have that!"

Our life paths had criss-crossed so often in the last few months; it had to be more than co-incidence. 'Everything happens for a reason'. Jessica's voice echoed around the threads as they weaved through my head. Were we destined to meet? Was this fated?

"There's something else," Connor said, turning me to face him. "Dean."

"What about him?" My skin tingled under his

touch, his blue eyes hypnotised me.

"It seems likely he is my son."

My hand covered my open-mouthed shock.

"Does he know?" Guilt rippled over me. "He said he needed to talk to me. I— when did— how— Fuck!"

"Yeah, that's pretty much how I took it," said Connor laughing, "but he took it much better. He's a fantastic kid."

"I knew he was special. He's another strand to… this. Whatever 'this' is."

"Look, what do you say we go to mine, I'll make us something to eat," suggested Connor, "we can try and make some sense of this web that's woven around us."

"I'm not sure I'm up to going out," I smoothed down my ruffled ponytail.

"You don't need to, I live on the next floor down, in fact – going by the view – I live right below you. You can close your mouth, that's the last revelation, for now."

CHAPTER 25

Connor shifted his weight from one foot to the other, clicking his fingers. I smoothed the collar of his navy suit jacket and straightened his purple tie. His aftershave billowed around me. Seventy-five days since he had picked me up; figuratively, and literally.

"Relax," I soothed, "these people have paid to see you, and they want to hear your story."

He had been an easy sell. Handsome, ex-military, strong yet vulnerable, with a story that tugged the hardest of hearts. He smirked.

"What's running through that pretty head of yours?" he asked, slipping his arms around me.

"I was thinking how handsome you are." I put my arms around his neck. "If you were ugly I wouldn't have been able to charge as much for the tickets."

"I'm offended." He feigned shock. "I am so much more than a piece of meat Miss Harvey."

"Indeed you are." I kissed him, wiping my lip gloss off his mouth. "You're my life saver."

He squeezed me to him and nuzzled my neck, his warm breath sent shivers through me.

"I need to go and take my seat, listen for Kaitlin introducing you. Good Luck!"

Kaitlin addressed the audience. She thanked them for attending, outlined the evening, and introduced Connor. I tiptoed out of the wings, along the front row of seats, and slipped in between Dean and Andrew. Andrew smiled and squeezed my hand. The stage was set with a couple of cream leather armchairs. Between them, on a side table stood a beautiful array of Forget-me-nots, and a framed picture of Jessica. Kaitlin walked as she talked.

"… Jessica Nelson was an amazing woman, who is greatly missed, and we are honoured tonight to be joined by her husband, Andrew, as we celebrate the launch of her final project.

"'How Will You Remember Me?' is Belfast born Connor Maxwell's autobiography. It takes us through the adventures of his childhood, his working life travelling around the world, and the heart-breaking loss of his identical twin brother. The story of how this book came to publication could easily be another novel. Ladies and Gentlemen, I am delighted to welcome Mr Connor Maxwell."

Connor walked on to the stage, bowing his head to

the audience. He kissed Kaitlin's cheek and waited for her to sit before he did. Damn, he looked good. He wore a suit so well, and his blue shirt was the exact colour of his eyes. I imagined women falling head over heels around me, and allowed myself a moment of smugness.

He had unlocked me. The first time I laid eyes on him, he had turned the key, allowing me to open the door and release my fears. When he picked me up off the street, I was at my most vulnerable, yet I had never worried about him hurting me. He was my saviour, my strength. My soul mate.

Kaitlin fielded questions from the audience, touched on poignant parts of the book, without giving too much away, and let Connor have his voice.

"I have so many people to thank for getting me here today Kaitlin, including yourself, for whipping my writing into a legible state." Connor flashed a devastating smile. "I have to thank Jessica for taking a chance on me, and allowing me to tell my story, and also for giving me a valuable piece of advice. To have a little faith in fate, and to remember that everything happens for a reason. Everything.

"In this world of fact, and reason, and logic, the concept of fate, of destiny, is somewhat scorned. In fact, I told her I thought it was 'wishy-washy', but knowing what I do now, I believe. In fact, the book needs another chapter to cover the last six months.

"I suffered a horrendous loss, the other half of me, a pain I can't put into words. However, I have also gained. A son. A son who has grown into an amazing young man, despite his own losses. And while I may have arrived late, it was better than never.

"I have also met an incredible woman, and even though we kept missing each other, fate brought me back to her again, and again. So while the loss of my brother was…" Connor paused, his hand on his chest as he blinked back tears. "… heart-breaking, if he hadn't have been sick I would still be working overseas, and would never have known about my son, Dean, or met Catherine."

"What has taught you the most valuable lesson in your life Connor, and how does it influence you?" Kaitlin asked.

The room was hushed in anticipation.

"Being in the army you learn to accept death. You accept the knowledge you could die at any time, for any reason.

"As a society, we get so lost in the bullshit, and all the monotonous crap people worry about. The fact is everyone dies, but few people live.

"We should be endlessly searching for new experiences, learning new things. Forging friendships with people who can teach us, and challenge us. We should demand more from life, and from ourselves. We should be striving to achieve, so we may live on after death. So we will be remembered."

I was on the eve of my 40th birthday, facing a different life to the one I expected to have six months ago. Jack had gone. Jessica gone, too. I ached for her, but I was grateful for having her in my life, for the connection we had shared, and the richness knowing her had given me. While I couldn't accept that their deaths could be reasoned, Jack's death had allowed me to open up, and Jessica's had brought me Connor. I had a chance of a family with him, and his son.

One thing I knew for sure, I would always have faith in fate.

ABOUT THE AUTHOR

Janine Cobain moved to Belfast in 2005, from the northeast of England. Having always been a prolific reader, she recently rekindled her love of writing, and How Will You Remember Me? is her first novel.

"I wear many hats – wife, mother, grandmother, writer, reader, manager – but underneath them all, I am me.

Find Janine on Facebook

www.facebook.com/JanineCobainAuthor

And Twitter

@JC2703

Write Path NI Limited are an independent publishing company based in Belfast, and we are always interested in new talent. Email us;

submissions@writepathni.com

Also Available From Write Path NI Limited

VOLUNTEER by GARY McELKERNEY

Chris Johnston, a 22 year old university student from Belfast, signs away another summer to lead a team of young volunteers as they travel to Ethiopia to build houses for charity. After an argument with the other leaders, Chris abandons the team and travels north to work for Medical Aid Africa in a clinic close to the Eritrean border. He agrees to join their make-shift ambulance crew in a bid to find the excitement he's been searching for on the frontline, but finds life very different off the beaten track. Consumed by fear, he is terrified and experiences the true horrors of war as his dreams of heroism and adventure turn into a nightmare. Volunteer is laced with humour, heartbreak and horror and Chris' journey will leave you questioning your own life, your achievements. If faced with the same situations, what would you do? And if the mental scars of war were carved into your memories, who would save you?

www.writepathni.com/shop

Also Available From Write Path NI Limited

SCATTERED HEART by ROISIN
DONNELLY

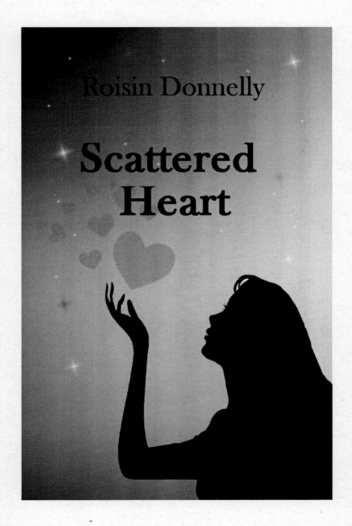

Scattered Heart is Roisin Donnelly's first collection of poetry. The acutely personal writing style gives you a voyeuristic insight into her experiences, and the powerful words bring depth to the pain, joy, and confusion of love, life, and loss. The paperback version of this beautifully unique book encourages you to document your own thoughts, feelings, and inspirations as you wander through the words that have come straight from her heart.

www.writepathni.com/shop